GOLD IS OUT TO DESTROY THE WHOLE VAINMILL SYNDICATE!

"He doesn't give a damn about the *Velvet Comet*! It's Vainmill he's after," the Syndicate's new chairman said.

"The stuff he stole can only be used against the *Comet*."

The chairman sighed wearily, looking in disgust at the man who was supposed to be her top troubleshooter. "How can you be so foolish when you're trying to be so clever? If he just wanted to close down the *Comet*, he'd lobby to make prostitution illegal in the Deluros system, and if he got desperate enough, he'd find a way to plant a bomb up there. But look at what he stole: holographic records of the faeries' training sessions. He wants to destroy Vainmill because of our exploitation of alien races; to him, the *Velvet Comet* is just a temporary battlefield. But now that he's declared war, Gold is going to find out just how dangerous a battlefield the *Comet* can really be. . . ."

Ø

Take a ride on the starship Signet

TALES OF THE VELVET COMET #3

EROS DESCENDING

A SCIENCE FICTION NOVEL

MIKE RESNICK

A SIGNET BOOK

NEW AMERICAN LIBRARY

NAL BOOKS ARE AVAILABLE AT QUANTITY DISCOUNTS WHEN
USED TO PROMOTE PRODUCTS OR SERVICES. FOR INFORMA-
TION PLEASE WRITE TO PREMIUM MARKETING DIVISION, NEW
AMERICAN LIBRARY, 1633 BROADWAY, NEW YORK, NEW YORK
10019.

Copyright © 1985 by Mike Resnick

Cover art by Kevin Johnson

SIGNET TRADEMARK REG. U.S. PAT. OFF. AND FOREIGN COUNTRIES
REGISTERED TRADEMARK—MARCA REGISTRADA
HECHO EN CHICAGO, U.S.A.

SIGNET, SIGNET CLASSIC, MENTOR, PLUME, MERIDIAN AND NAL BOOKS
are published by New American Library,
1633 Broadway, New York, New York 10019

First Printing, December, 1985

1 2 3 4 5 6 7 8 9

PRINTED IN THE UNITED STATES OF AMERICA

To Carol, as always,

and to Tom Easton,
for criticism and encouragement

PROLOGUE

The *Velvet Comet* spun slowly in space, resembling nothing more than a giant barbell. Its metal skin glistened a brilliant silver, and its array of flashing lights could be seen from literally tens of thousands of miles away.

Seventeen different engineering firms had worked on its design, thousands of men and machines had spent millions of hours on its construction, and it housed a permanent staff of more than six hundred men and women. Owned and financed by the Vainmill Syndicate, the largest of the Republic's conglomerates, it had been built in orbit around the distant planet of Charlemagne, but now it circled Deluros VIII, the huge world that would someday become the capital planet of the race of Man.

During its eighty-seven years of existence it had become a byword for opulence and elegance, a synonym for hedonism and dissipation. Its fame had spread to the most remote worlds of the Republic, and while its sybaritic luxuries and even its air of exclusivity were often imitated, they were never equaled.

The *Velvet Comet*, after more than three decades of gestation, had been born in space, and less than a century after its birth it would die in space, mourned by few and forgotten by most. But in the meantime, it did its living with a grace and style that would not be seen again for many millennia.

It was the crown jewel in the Syndicate's Entertainment and Leisure Division, a showplace where the rich and the famous—and occasionally the notorious—gathered to see and be seen, to conspicuously consume, and to revel in pleasures which were designed to satisfy even the most jaded of tastes. For while the *Velvet Comet* housed a compendium of the finest shops and boutiques, of gourmet restaurants and elegant lounges, while it boasted a fabulous casino and a score of other entertainments, it was first and foremost a brothel.

And it was the brothel, and the promises of secret delights that it proffered, that enticed its select clientele out to the *Comet*. They came from Deluros VIII and a thousand nearby and distant worlds. Money was no object to these men and women; they came to play, and to relax, and to indulge.

All except one of them, who came with one purpose in mind, and left with another.

1

The tall, elegantly clad, blond woman reached out a jeweled hand and rubbed Secretariat's foreface, as the muscular chestnut colt pawed nervously at the bedding of his makeshift stall. His groom, leaning against one of the storage area's walls, kept a watchful eye on the sleek red horse.

"He's lovely," said the Steel Butterfly.

"He's about as pretty a horse as I've ever had in my charge," agreed the groom.

"Very well behaved, too," she continued. "Especially considering how strange his surroundings must seem to him." The Steel Butterfly stroked Secretariat's long, arching neck. "You know, I've never seen a horse before."

"Not too many people in the Deluros system have," said the groom. "They're mostly confined to Earth and some of the other worlds out on the Rim."

"When did he run?"

"You mean the first time he lived? Oh, maybe a couple of thousand years ago."

She stared at the colt in awe. "And people still remember him? Amazing!"

"He was one of the ones," said the groom. "I've had the Australian Eclipse from the twenty-second century, and Hawkmaster from the twenty-sixth, but I'd have to say that he's the best I've ever rubbed down."

The Steel Butterfly smiled. "I wish I'd had the same quality in the animals *I've* rubbed down."

"You've rubbed animals?" asked the groom, mildly surprised.

"Thousands of them," she replied, then added with a wry grimace: "Mostly men."

The groom merely stared at her, then looked past her to a corridor. "We've got company," he said.

"I knew it was too good to last," she muttered, turning in the direction he had indicated.

Two men, one speaking with great animation, the other listening with an expression of distaste and boredom, were approaching the storage area. The shorter one was a bit overweight, but carefully and expensively dressed to hide the fact, or at least diminish its effect. His artificial hair glowed all the colors of the rainbow, and his fingers were so laden with rings that they seemed more jewel than flesh. Nonetheless, the Steel Butterfly's eyes were drawn to the conservatively dressed taller man, whose carriage and manner seemed to reflect an easy confidence and an aura of authority. His lean face was austere and craggy, the features sharp and finely chiseled. His straight black hair was edged with gray, and his hands were starting to spot with age, but there was a spring to his step that made him appear younger than his fifty plus years.

"Ah, there you are!" said Gustave Plaga, extending a ring-covered hand in the Steel Butterfly's direction, but stopping some ten feet short of her. "I had a feeling we'd find you here." He gestured ingratiatingly toward the taller man. "May I present the Reverend Thomas Gold?"

"I've seen you so often on the video I feel as if I know you personally, Reverend Gold," said the Steel Butterfly.

Gold smiled tightly. "A simple *Doctor* Gold will do," he replied. "Mr. Plaga tells me that you're the manager of this establishment."

"The madam," the Steel Butterfly corrected him.

"Yes," said Gold. He turned his attention to Secretariat. "This one's nice and calm, I see. Not like that black one I just visited in the cargo area. He's practically tearing the ship apart."

"He'll be all right," interjected the groom. "It's just his manner."

"Are you quite certain?" asked Gold dubiously. "He's doing everything short of snorting smoke and belching fire."

The groom nodded. "I've seen him before. He's always like that—high-spirited."

"I would have called it psychotic." Gold shrugged. "Well, I suppose I'll have to take your word for it. These are the first two racehorses I've seen."

There was a momentary silence.

Plaga cleared his throat. "I'm afraid I have to see to some of our other VIPs." He turned to the Steel Butterfly. "So if you will continue Doctor Gold's tour . . ." He fidgeted uncomfortably.

"Certainly," said the Steel Butterfly. "But first

I'd like to go over a few details of this afternoon's schedule with you."

Gold, who had been watching them both, seemed amused. "Don't mind me," he said. "This is the first time all day that I haven't been surrounded by Vainmill executives. I'll be happy to spend a few minutes petting the horse." He looked at the groom. "If it is permitted, that is?"

The groom shrugged. "Suit yourself. I don't mind if he doesn't."

"Fine," said the Steel Butterfly, following Plaga around a bend in the corridor. "I'll be back in just a moment."

"No hurry," said Gold, rubbing the chestnut colt's neck.

"All right, Gustave," she said coldly when they had walked some fifty feet up the corridor. "What the hell is the big idea?"

"I've had him all morning," complained Plaga.

"That's your job."

"My job is running the Entertainment and Leisure Division," said Plaga. "And that son of a bitch"—he jerked his thumb in Gold's direction—"has been taking potshots at me on video every Friday night for five years. Three hours of him is about all I can take."

"This whole thing was your idea, Gustave," said the Steel Butterfly. "The least you can do is follow through on it."

"Look," he said nervously. "I've got to get away for about forty minutes. Important things are happening."

"Such as?"

"It's nothing you need concern yourself with," said Plaga.

"Everything that happens aboard the *Comet* concerns me, Gustave," said the Steel Butterfly. "What's going on?"

"Just see that he enjoys himself, and I'll tell you all about it later," said Plaga, checking his time-piece anxiously.

"Just see that he enjoys himself?" she repeated sarcastically. "Damm it, Gustave, who do you think he is? The Jesus Pures think *music* is immoral, for Christ's sake! They don't eat meat, they don't drink coffee, they probably screw by proxy—and he's not just *any* Jesus Pure. He's their goddamned leader! Now, exactly what kind of good time do you think I ought to show him?"

Plaga checked his timepiece again.

"I can't waste any more time arguing with you," he said. "I'll be forty minutes—an hour, tops. That's not asking too damned much, is it?"

She stared at him. "I just hope whatever you're doing is half as important as you think it is."

"It is," he said, relieved. "Keep him in a good mood."

She uttered a sardonic laugh, turned on her heel, and returned to the storage area.

"I'm sorry to have kept you waiting," she said to Gold when she arrived.

"It's quite all right," replied Gold. "Given a choice between Vainmill executives and a horse, I'll take the horse every time." He stopped stroking Secretariat's muzzle. "Did Plaga make a graceful escape?"

"Not very," admitted the Steel Butterfly.

"Well, he wasn't the most graceful man I've ever met," said Gold contemptuously. He looked directly at her. "What now?"

She smiled. "Now I keep you amused until he gets back from wherever he's gone."

"That may be a little harder than you think," said Gold.

"So I've been given to understand," replied the Steel Butterfly. "I gather we've got about an hour to kill. Would you care to have lunch?"

"I just finished a so-called prayer breakfast with eighteen Vainmill officers," said Gold. "They served me bacon and eggs, which I can't eat, and I served them up some truth that I suspect *they* couldn't swallow. I think one such experience per day is more than sufficient."

"We have a number of very fine restaurants on the *Comet*," she said. "I won't order for you and you needn't pray for me." She smiled. "That might make things more palatable."

"No, thank you. I'm not hungry, and I make it a habit not to patronize restaurants that serve slaughtered animals."

"We could simply stay down here," suggested the Steel Butterfly.

"I think not," said Gold. "I am not an immodest man, but it would be unrealistic to assume that my presence here is not the subject of considerable attention. I don't think it would look very good for you and me to be absent together for any period of time."

"Even if we just pet the horse?"

"For a man in my position there is very little difference between the appearance of impropriety and impropriety itself. I think that spending an hour out of the public's sight in the company of the *Velvet Comet*'s madam would be a bad idea."

She shrugged. "Whatever you say—but I'm going to need some help from you."

He frowned. "What kind of help?"

"I assume that you have no interest in seeing

our suites, or our fantasy rooms, or our casino, or our bars, or our nightclubs ... so you'll have to tell me what you *are* willing to look at."

"Is there anything left?" he asked.

"Not too much," she admitted. "The hydroponics garden, the hospital, the public rooms, and the Mall."

"The Mall? Isn't that the shopping area?"

She nodded. "It's also where we'll be holding the race."

"Let's start with the public rooms," he said. "I wouldn't want anyone to think I was shopping here."

"We have many fine shops and boutiques in the Mall," she replied. "Including a brokerage house, an antiquarian bookstore, a number of jewelers and art dealers ..."

"You also sell liquor, drugs, tobacco, and clothing designed for sexual enticement," said Gold. "I would prefer to go to the public rooms until the race is about to start."

"As you wish," said the Steel Butterfly. She walked over to Secretariat and gave his neck a fond pat. "Good luck, horse. Give him hell."

"He'll do that," the groom assured her.

"Come on," said the Steel Butterfly, leading Gold down the corridor to an elevator. "If I stay down here any longer, I'm going to adopt him."

They emerged into the crowded reception foyer, an elegant room that held some three hundred people comfortably and was now coping with almost five hundred people—patrons, prostitutes of both sexes, VIPs, and security personnel. A number of crystal chandeliers had been imported from Earth itself, though they were strictly ornamental, as the room was illuminated very efficiently by a hidden lighting system. The carpet was a hand-woven alien fabric, plush and resilient, with delicate and intricate patterns repeating endlessly in various pastels. The chairs and couches were both ornate and comfortable, and a number of exquisite holographs, some originals, some reproductions, lined the walls. One corner housed a bank of computer screens that continuously updated the latest political, business, and sports news, and an extra half-dozen computer terminals had been temporarily moved in to handle bets on the upcoming race. Waiters and waitresses circulated among the clusters of people, offering free drinks and exotic edibles.

"It's impressive, I'll grant you that," remarked Gold, glancing around the foyer with a mixture of fascination and distaste. "I can't help wondering what good some of the money that was spent decorating this place might have done out on the frontier worlds."

The Steel Butterfly shook her head as a waiter approached them. "Vainmill has a number of projects on the Inner Frontier," she replied, raising her voice to be heard over the conversations of the clustered patrons.

"Nonsense," said Gold, glaring at a middle-aged woman, laden with diamonds and a dress that was just a bit too small for her, as she inadvertently bumped into him. "I was born in the Meritonia System. I *saw* what they did, and I've been fighting them ever since."

"You're referring to the affair on New Capri?" she asked.

"Among other things."

"I thought they made restitution for that."

"How do you make restitution for wiping out an entire alien population?" he demanded.

"I understand that it was accidental," said the Steel Butterfly.

"Destroying a populated planet's ecology so you can turn it into a giant smelting plant is hardly accidental," said Gold passionately. "Not that New Capri is the only example of Vainmill's venality. Their exploitation of alien races out on the frontier is well documented."

"And yet, here you are at Vainmill's most luxurious showplace," noted the Steel Butterfly with a smile.

"Every sinner has a cross to bear," replied Gold. "I'm Vainmill's," he added purposefully.

"It might not look that way to the casual observer," she said dryly.

"Of course not," he agreed. "I never said Vainmill was stupid; just evil. This whole charity festival was arranged solely to get me up here this weekend."

"It sounds to me, Doctor Gold, as if you're guilty of the sin of pride. We're giving the weekend's earnings to fifteen different churches and charities."

"Not pride; just realism. Everything else is window dressing. I'm the one who's been attacking them from the pulpit for the past five years; I'm the one they set this up for."

"Then why did you come?" she asked curiously, stepping aside to let a group of eight patrons and their companions pass by.

"Because I can't be bought off—though I'm perfectly willing to let them try," he replied. "Make a ten-million-credit contribution to the Church of the Purity of Jesus Christ every day, and I'll be up here to hand out a trophy to the owner of the winning horse every day. Make it twenty, and I'll

take the Lodin XI ambassador's place at the raffle
and draw the winning number."

"I would have thought you'd frown upon such
unclean money," remarked the Steel Butterfly.

"The uses I put it to will cleanse it."

"Then you should be the happiest man on the
Comet."

"My dear woman," he said, "I don't underestimate your intelligence; please don't underestimate
mine." He paused to take a deep breath. "Do you
think I don't know that you have half a dozen
cameras trained on me as I stand here speaking to
the most famous madam in the Republic, or that
my followers won't be subjected to numerous holographs of me surrounded by Vainmill executives and suggestively-clad prostitutes?" He drew
himself up to his full height, a look of contempt
crossing his face. "Does Vainmill think they've
bought me off? Do they really think my people
can't see through this ruse as easily as I can? I
arrived in a state of Grace, and I will leave in a
state of Grace. A little humiliation is a small price
to pay for the good that that money can do. Jesus,
too, walked among sinners; I can do no less." He
paused, and seemed to relax. "So I'll preside at
your horserace, and I'll distribute your money to
the needy, and I'll let Vainmill prove their virtue
by shutting down the *Velvet Comet*—and I'd love to
see Plaga's face when he hears my sermon next
Friday."

"Just a moment," said the Steel Butterfly. "What
was that you just said about shutting down the
Comet?"

"I said that it won't do them a bit of good," he
replied firmly. "The *Comet* is just a symptom;
Vainmill is the disease."

"Has someone actually told you that they plan to close the *Comet*?" she persisted, lowering her voice as she became aware of the curious stares she was attracting from a number of nearby patrons.

"Not directly—but it's Vainmill's logical next step, after giving the money to my church doesn't work. After all, this is the one Vainmill business that makes no bones about reveling in sin."

"Kill the *Comet*, just to shut you up?" she said incredulously. "You have an awfully inflated opinion of yourself, Doctor Gold!"

He stared calmly at her and made no comment.

"I don't believe it," she continued.

"What you believe is immaterial," he said with a shrug.

"It sounds like one of Gustave's idiot ideas."

"Plaga is just a flunky."

"He's the president of the Entertainment and Leisure Division," said the Steel Butterfly.

"I told you: I'm not after a division. I'm after *Vainmill*. Whether the *Comet* survives a month or a year or a decade is a matter of complete indifference to me—except, of course, that it's an abomination that ought to be terminated for its own excesses."

"Has it occured to you that this abomination employs more than eight hundred people, and that killing the *Comet* would throw them out of work?"

"I am not such an egomaniac that I believe shutting down the *Comet* will eradicate all sin everywhere," replied Gold. "I have no doubt that all your beautiful young men and women will be employed within a week—though I'll certainly do my best to prevent it."

"You won't prevent it," she said.

"Probably not," he admitted.

"But what you *will* do," she continued, "is send them out onto the streets of Deluros VIII and other worlds, where they'll require the consent and protection of the criminal element to ply their trade, where their working conditions will no longer be under the control of skilled medics, where—"

"Are you trying to tell me," he interrupted with a sardonic smile, "that only prostitutes who work aboard the *Velvet Comet* receive medical attention?"

"Doctor Gold, more than four hundred venereal diseases have been discovered since Man went out to the stars. Only the *Comet* has the facilities to instantly recognize and cure each of them."

"Then that is the misfortune of those who are foolish enough to become prostitutes or to have sexual congress with them."

"That's an inadequate answer," said the Steel Butterfly. "Since you grant that Man always has and always will support prostitution, why not allow him to do so in a controlled and luxurious enviroment?"

"Sugar-coating sin doesn't make it any less sinful, only more caloric." He gestured toward the crowded room. "Look at these people. Are they any less sinful because they pay millions of credits to you and wear formal dress and dine on fine foods before partaking of the *Comet*'s pleasures? The only difference between them and a cargo loader who seeks quick and inexpensive satisfaction is what they pay, not what they do."

"By the same token, why don't you lead your crusade against all the top-rated restaurants that serve meat?"

"Because the Jesus Pures' refusal to eat meat is

a matter of personal choice, nothing more," Gold replied. "The Bible does not direct us to avoid meat. The same cannot be said of what goes on aboard the *Comet*." He paused. "Besides, I'm not crusading against the *Comet*, except as it relates to Vainmill. In fact, I doubt that I've mentioned it five times in the past year. If Vainmill offers it as a sop to me, I'll take it, but if they think I will stop or even moderate my attacks on them, they're sadly mistaken."

"You keep saying that they're going to kill the *Comet*," she said irritably. "If you really believed that, I would think that the madam is the last person you'd forewarn."

"It makes no difference," said Gold. "I am a moral man; I cannot be bought. Vainmill is an immoral corporation; they will continue to try to buy me, raising their price each time, on the assumption that *everyone* can be bought. Eventually it will bring about their downfall."

"You don't really think you can bring a corporation like Vainmill to its knees, do you?" she asked, amazed by the scope of his ego.

"One properly motivated man can bring down an empire," he replied seriously. "No one would remember David if Goliath had been a dwarf."

"You realize that if you actually succeeded, you'd do untold harm to the economy, as well as putting literally tens of millions of people out of work."

"Your loyalty is misplaced," said Gold. "Vainmill would cut the *Comet* loose in two seconds if they thought it would get me off their backs."

"And what of the ensuing financial upheaval if you destroy Vainmill?"

"The Republic will survive, just as the Earth survived forty days and forty nights of flooding.

And if it doesn't, then it wasn't built to last, and something better will supersede it."

"It must be comforting to be so absolutely certain that you're right," she said cynically.

"God vouchsafes precious few comforts to us," he replied. "That happens to be one of them."

"And if you're wrong?"

He met her gaze and spoke with the same degree of conviction with which he had outlined his future plans. "Then I will spend all of eternity in the pits of hell, suffering the tortures of the damned."

"You really believe that?" asked the Steel Butterfly.

"I do."

"Then why take the chance?"

"Because I believe that when God gave Man free will, it was implicit in the contract that he exercise it."

"And what of all the people who exercise it aboard the *Comet*?"

"The very nature of free will implies that Man is also free to abuse God's laws. Your patrons have made their choice, and I have made mine."

"You're as slick in person as you are on the video," she admitted begrudgingly. "I think it might be best to change the subject."

"As you wish."

"The race is due to start in about half an hour. Shall we start making our way to the presenter's platform?"

"Why not?" he assented.

Just then there was a small beeping sound, and the Steel Butterfly touched a tiny jewel on one of her bracelets.

"Yes?" she said softly.

"I regret to inform you that we have a scheduling problem," said a masculine voice.

"I'm occupied at the moment. You take care of it, Cupid." She touched the jewel again, then turned back to Gold. "I apologize for the interruption."

"Cupid?" he repeated.

"Our main computer."

"You've got a computer arranging liaisons?"

"No, but it keeps track of them. I don't know who gave it its name, but it seems appropriate. We equipped it with a voice about ten years ago."

"Interesting. What else does it do?"

"Other than the usual?" she replied. "Well, for one thing, it reports on any behavior that seems out of the ordinary."

"How can a machine determine aberrant behavior in a place like this?" asked Gold, honestly curious.

"With eighty-seven years of memory to draw on, it's pretty good at differentiating," answered the Steel Butterfly.

"So you've turned your computer into a voyeur," he remarked dryly. "It seems that even machines get corrupted by Vainmill."

"If that's what you'd like to believe," she said. "Of course, if someone turns Cupid off, you won't be able to breathe and you'll float away like a feather on the wind, but you'll have saved it from having to observe obscene acts."

He was about to reply when her bracelet beeped again.

"Yes, Cupid? What is it?"

"I regret that I am unable to solve the scheduling conflict," said the computer.

She sighed. "All right. What's the problem?"

"The Undersecretary of the Navy and her chosen companion had reserved the Mountaintop for two hours, commencing three minutes ago."

"Are the holographic projectors malfunctioning again?" asked the Steel Butterfly.

"No. But the group currently occupying the room refuses to vacate the premises."

"Tell them they have to."

"I have done so."

She frowned. "Are you telling me that our prostitutes are willfully ignoring your directives?"

"No. The room is occupied solely by eighteen executives from the Vainmill Syndicate, including the chairman and all the department heads, each of whom has the necessary clearance to override my commands."

"How long have they been there?"

"Forty-two minutes."

"Check with Gustave Plaga and see how much longer they'll be using the room."

"I have been forbidden to communicate with them again."

"What's going on there?" she demanded.

"I have been forbidden to say."

"But it's in your memory banks?"

"Yes," answered Cupid.

"I'll check them later," she said. "In the meantime, offer the Undersecretary our apologies, tell her there will be no charge for the weekend, and if the Demolition Team is available, see if she'd like them to visit her."

She pressed the jewel again.

"Demolition Team?" asked Gold.

"You don't want to know," she replied.

"I suppose not," he agreed. "What's the Mountaintop?"

"A room designed to resemble a ski lodge atop

the tallest mountain on Mirzam X. The projectors give it a panoramic view of the surrounding mountain range."

"Interesting," said Gold. "You've figured out what they're doing in there, haven't you?"

"Selling the *Comet* out?" she said sarcastically.

"That would be premature," said Gold. "But they're certainly trying to decide whether the *Comet* is a sufficient bone to toss to me, or whether I'm going to want more."

"My guess is that they're probably thinking up ways to fight you," she responded as she led him through the crowded foyer toward the entrance to the Mall.

"I doubt it. They've been singularly ineffective for the past five years."

"Then perhaps they're looking for your fatal flaw," she suggested. "Everybody has one, you know—even you."

"True," he agreed, stepping out into the Mall. "But whatever mine may be," he continued confidently, "I think I can safely state that the last place it's likely to manifest itself is aboard the *Velvet Comet*."

2

There was carefully spread dirt as far as the eye could see.

"Watch your step," cautioned the Steel Butterfly, as they skirted a temporary restraining rail and made their way to a slidewalk.

"Just how big is this place?" asked Gold, looking off into the distance but unable to see the end of the Mall.

"A little over two miles," she replied. "Both sides are lined with shops and boutiques from here to the main airlock, which is about two-thirds of the way down the strip. Past the airlock are storage areas, our hospital, maintenance supplies, Security headquarters, and some more stores." She turned to him and smiled. "We even have a non-denominational chapel. Perhaps you'd like to visit it?"

"I think I'll forgo the privilege," said Gold as he reached the crowded slidewalk and stepped onto it. "They ought to make these things wider," he muttered as a pair of young women brushed by him and got off at a shop that specialized in garments made from the skins of alien animals.

"See this parquet flooring?" said the Steel Butterfly, pointing to a ten-foot strip between the slidewalk and the restraining rail. "We left a strip bare so that the dirt couldn't get into the slidewalk mechanism. Actually, it goes all the way across the middle of the Mall to the other slidewalk—when it's not covered by racetrack, that is. Many of our patrons prefer walking to riding." She looked distastefully at the makeshift track and sighed. "I certainly don't envy Maintenance. They're going to have to clean up three hundred tons of this stuff."

"That much?"

"It seems a shame to use it only once," commented the Steel Butterfly, as the slidewalk took them past a trio of boutiques, an antique shop, and a brokerage house. As they approached a shop that sold imported flowers, she saw a video technician perched atop a ladder, positioning a holographic camera.

"What's the problem up there?" she asked him, as she and Gold stepped off the slidewalk when it reached the flower shop. "I thought everything was supposed to be ready by last night."

"They moved the finish line," answered the man with a grimace. "Evidently it takes racehorses quite a while to come to a stop, and they didn't want them running into any walls. So now all the cameras have to be repositioned."

"Where's the finish line now?" asked the Steel Butterfly.

"About three hundred yards farther from the Resort than it was. We've already moved the grandstand and the presentation platform."

"Can't they just run a shorter distance?"

The man shrugged. "I must have spent an hour arguing that very point with their trainers. You would have thought I had suggested vivisecting them. The gist of it is that a mile and a quarter was the classic distance the first time they lived, and that's what they've been conditioned to run." He paused. "It's a pain in the ass. You'd think animals as famous as these two would be more adaptable."

She turned back to Gold as the two of them stepped back onto the slidewalk.

"You look disapproving," she remarked.

"I have the distinct impression that it's against the laws of God and Nature," he replied.

"The distance?" she asked with a laugh.

"The resurrection of these animals."

"Against God's, perhaps, but not Nature's. Once science discovered DNA coding, it was only a matter of time before they started preserving cell samples in liquid nitrogen against the day they could reproduce them."

"I know how it's done," he told her. "They've been wanting to reproduce Men that way for more than a century. So far we've been able to stop them from passing the necessary legislation."

"So you prefer the way we do it aboard the *Comet*?"

"Don't be clever with me," said Gold. "It's unbecoming."

"I wasn't aware that the Jesus Pures had a monopoly on clever answers," she said.

"On *correct* answers."

The Steel Butterfly stared at him for a moment, then sighed and shrugged.

"Anyway," she said, returning to what she hoped

was a less controversial subject, "these were supposed to be the two best racehorses of their era. At least, the press has been going crazy all month long." She paused. "I've never seen a horserace. I hope it's as exciting as they say."

"One would think that there was more than enough excitement up here already," said Gold caustically, as they passed an expensive lingerie shop.

Suddenly his attention was captured by two small figures emerging from an art gallery that specialized in paintings from Earth. "I wasn't aware that you allowed children aboard the *Velvet Comet*," he said with a disapproving frown.

"We don't."

"Then what are *those*?" he demanded, pointing to the undersized figures.

"Faeries," she replied.

"That was a serious question."

"It was a serious answer. Officially, they're members of the Andrican race of Besmarith II. But they look like they're right out of Spenser's *The Faerie Queene*, so that's what we call them."

"I didn't realize that the *Velvet Comet* catered to aliens."

She shook her head. "They're not patrons, Doctor Gold."

"You mean they *work* here?"

"Perhaps you'd like to meet them. You might find them interesting."

Before he could answer her, she had caught the aliens' attention, and they approached her with an inhuman grace.

Each of them stood a few inches under five feet in height, with shimmering silvery skins, opalescent feathery hair, wide-set oversized sky-blue eyes, permanently arched eyebrows, pointed ears, and an overall look of almost mythic innocence to them. Only when they got to within ten feet could Gold discern that the smaller of the two was a male, while the other, whose budding breasts were barely visible beneath her translucent alien garment, was a female. Neither possessed the hardened musculature of adults, though upon closer inspection it was obvious that they weren't quite children, either. They were barefoot, and Gold, when he could finally tear his curious gaze away from their faces, saw that their feet were three-toed and webbed.

"This is Oberon," said the Steel Butterfly, gesturing to the male. "And this is Titania."

Titania opened her mouth to say something; it came out as a series of melodic trilling whistles.

The Steel Butterfly frowned. "You forgot them again. How many times have I spoken to you about that?"

Titania trilled again.

The Steel Butterfly turned to Gold. "They're continually leaving their translating devices behind," she explained. "And while they may sound very pretty, no one can understand anything they're saying."

"They seem to understand you."

"Oh, they understand Terran perfectly. It's a much simpler language than Andrican. But they can't pronounce a word of it." She turned back to the two pixielike aliens. "All right—but as soon as the race is over, I want to see both of you with your devices."

Oberon whistled something, making a fuller, deeper sound than had Titania, smiled boyishly at her, and then the two of them glided off, hand in hand.

"And humans actually have sex with them?" asked Gold, his expression a mixture of fascination and distaste.

"They've been among our most popular employees for the five years they've been working here."

"Five years?" he repeated unbelievingly. "They look so . . . *fresh.*"

"I suppose that's why they're so popular. We've tried to recruit more members of their race, but so far we haven't had very much luck."

"How did you come by these two?"

"I gather their family owed a considerable debt to Vainmill—it had something to do with some trade concessions in the Alphard Cluster—and this was the solution. They're brother and sister, though they don't view the relationship quite the same way that we do."

"In other words," said Gold coldly, "they've been *forced* to work here."

The Steel Butterfly looked amused. "You'd have to force them to *stop*—which is why I can't understand why we've had such difficulty recruiting others of their race."

"View it as a small triumph for morality," said Gold. He continued staring as the petite aliens. "I've been fighting Vainmill over just this kind of exploitation for half my life. I know they still do it on the frontier worlds, but I never thought they'd have the unmitigated gall to think they could get away with this right here in the Deluros system!"

"I assure you, Doctor Gold—they are hardly being exploited. Their wages are substantial, and are on deposit in the *Comet*'s bank."

"Oh?" he said sharply. "What do they spend their money on?"

"I've no idea," she replied. "Almost all of their needs are provided for."

"Then I'll tell you," he said. "They don't spend it on anything, because they have no more knowledge of human economics than they have of human morality. And when they leave, Vainmill will sit on their money for seven years and then take ten minutes getting a friendly judge to rule that the accounts are dead and that they are entitled to both the money and the accrued interest. I've seen them work this all across the Inner Frontier."

"And what if they get an *un*friendly judge?" inquired the Steel Butterfly.

"They know the difference," said Gold wryly. "They own a goodly number of them."

"I'm afraid all of this is beyond my realm of experience," said the Steel Butterfly, trying to end the discussion. "My job is running a brothel."

"With pubescent children who haven't any idea of what they're doing!"

"I repeat: they *are* adults."

"They certainly don't look it—and I've no doubt that Vainmill capitalizes on that fact." He paused. "In retrospect, I don't know why I'm so surprised; it was perhaps the only sin Vainmill hadn't yet committed. I just wonder that any of your clientele has the lack of shame to request them."

"You'd be surprised at what some of our clientele have requested."

"I certainly hope I would." He paused. "You said you hadn't had any luck obtaining more of them?"

"I said we hadn't had *much* luck," she corrected him. "There are six more at our training school."

"You have a training school?" he asked, surprised.

She nodded. "I attended it myself before I came to work up here. It's run by a former madam named Suma. She must be, oh, in her eighties or nineties; the last time I saw her she was in rather poor health."

"And what kind of deal did Vainmill make to get six more of them?"

"I really couldn't say."

"Couldn't, or won't?"

"I meant what I said, Doctor Gold."

"Is there any prostitution on the faeries' home planet?"

"I've never heard any mention of it," replied the Steel Butterfly.

"I can't say that I'm surprised."

"I have a feeling that you're letting your religion color your viewpoint," said the Steel Butterfly. "You remarked earlier that they were innocent. Might I suggest that the only thing they're innocent of is your particular notion of morality?"

"I have never forced my morality upon an alien race that was incapable of comprehending it," said Gold. "But by the same token, Vainmill has no right to force its immorality on them."

"Even if they enjoy it?" asked the Steel Butterfly.

"We were speaking about free will a moment ago," said Gold. "If, after leaving the *Comet*, these two aliens were willingly to return to it, they'll have made their choice and will pay their penalty in the hereafter—but for Vainmill to preempt that choice by making it for them is unacceptable."

She sighed wearily but made no reply, and they rode the next fifty yards in silence.

Then Gustave Plaga stepped out of the reception foyer and began approaching them, walking rapidly on the narrow strip of exposed parquet flooring to bypass the crowded, slower-moving slidewalk. Gold and the Steel Butterfly also stepped onto the floor to greet him, and Gold spotted a number of Vainmill executives riding the slidewalk in his direction.

"I apologize for being gone so long, but it was unavoidable," said Plaga, more to the madam than to Gold. "I trust you've been enjoying yourself, Doctor Gold?"

"*Enjoy* is not exactly the word I would choose," replied Gold. "Let us say that I've found it quite enlightening."

"The race is due to start in about twenty minutes," said Plaga. "Why don't we take our seats now?"

Gold nodded his agreement, and they rode the slidewalk to the grandstand, which was only five rows deep but almost one hundred yards long, and fit neatly into the area between the retaining rail and the slidewalk. A few moments later they were seated in a comfortable box overlooking the finish line, directly adjacent to the presentation platform, where an ornate golden cup topped by a platinum racehorse was on display.

"I expected a larger crowd," commented Gold, gesturing to the small groups of men and women who were slowly wending their way to the long, narrow, makeshift grandstand.

"Oh, we'll draw about four thousand people," answered the Steel Butterfly.

"Where are they?"

"*I* would say they were enjoying the facilities. *You* would say they were sinning."

"*You* would be wrong," said Gold.

"Is there anything you haven't seen yet that you'd like us to show you?" asked Plaga.

"I think I've seen what I came to see."

"Oh?"

"When I arrived here I wasn't quite sure of Vainmill's weakest link. Now, thanks to my little tour, I am."

"You think you've found it up here?" asked Plaga, trying to keep the curiosity from his voice.

"No," answered Gold. "I *know* I've found it up here."

"May I ask just what you think you've discovered?"

"I'll tell you when I'm ready to," said Gold.

Plaga stared at him for a moment, then shrugged. "As a matter of fact, Vainmill has just made arrangements to get rid of its weakest link."

'And what do *you* think it is?"

Plaga grinned. "To borrow a phrase that is probably being uttered all over the Resort as we sit here, I'll show you mine if you'll show me yours."

"You know, Mr. Plaga," said Gold, "I think I liked you better when you were disgustingly servile."

"Servility's not my style," said Plaga.

"I would never have guessed," replied Gold. He smiled confidently. "I don't know exactly what you think you accomplished at your meeting in the Ski Lodge"—Plaga shot the Steel Butterfly a furious look—"but it won't do you a bit of good." Gold paused. "Do try to catch my broadcast next week. I think you might find it interesting."

"A lot might happen before then," said Plaga with what he hoped was a mysterious smile.

"Perhaps," said Gold. "But I think I can guarantee that a lot will happen *after* my broadcast."

More people began moving toward the grandstand, and in another moment Gold was completely surrounded by Vainmill executives, each of whom spoke to him cordially. When the last of them was seated he turned to Plaga.

"Have your holograph operators gotten enough yet?" he asked.

"I beg your pardon?" said Plaga.

"I'm referring to the fact that the only people sitting within thirty feet of me are Vainmill officers who seem determined to greet me like a long-lost brother, and a number of suggestively dressed prostitutes."

"As a matter of fact, more than half of our prostitutes are males," replied Plaga, making no attempt to dispute his charge.

"Ah—but they might look like customers if they got into the picture."

"Possibly the women will look like patrons," suggested Plaga.

"Unquestionably," replied Gold ironically.

"Instead of studiously ignoring them, you might strike up a conversation or two. Who knows? You might make some converts."

"I'll choose my own converts, thank you," said Gold.

The two faeries joined the growing crowd in the grandstand, and Gold turned his attention back to them.

"Do they have wings?" he asked at last.

"Who?" asked the Steel Butterfly.

"The faeries."

"No. Why?"

He shrugged. "They look like they should."

Suddenly there was a brief commotion at the far end of the Mall, and then a trumpeted call to the post was piped in over the sound system.

"Ladies and gentlemen," said an unseen announcer, "if you will direct your attention toward the starting gate, you will see the first of the two contestants coming onto the track."

Gold looked off to his right.

"I can't see a thing," he said.

"Here," said the Steel Butterfly, handing him a tiny pair of binoculars. "Use these."

He held them up to his eyes and focused on the large, sleek chestnut colt which was just emerging from an unseen lift and stepping onto the dirt surface.

"Welcome to the first running of the *Velvet Comet* Challenge Cup," continued the announcer.

A gray-haired woman suddenly approached the crowded grandstand, and a number of Vainmill executives immediately moved over to make room for her.

"Interesting," commented Gold softly, as she climbed up into the grandstand.

"What is?" asked the Steel Butterfly.

"That's Fiona Bradley, the head of the Resource and Development Division."

"What's so interesting about her?"

"She was late for the prayer breakfast this morning, and nobody even stood up when she entered the room," said Gold. "Now they suddenly part before her like the Red Sea."

"Do you draw some conclusion from this?" she asked him.

"No," he replied. "But it *is* interesting."

He put the binoculars back up to his eyes and looked down the track at the chestnut colt.

"This year's Challenge Cup, which will be presented to the winner by Doctor Thomas Gold," said the announcer, emphasizing the name, "features two of the great horses of the late twentieth century. Currently on the track, wearing the blue-and-gold silks of the Quantos Corporation, is Secretariat. Like his rival, he will carry one hundred and twenty-six pounds today." He droned on and on, listing the accomplishments of the original Secretariat, the two previous laboratory-created duplicates, and the present version. "This Secretariat is currently three years and eight months old."

"Isn't that awfully young?" asked Gold, curious in spite of himself.

"Actually, I gather that he's already nearing the end of his career," said the Steel Butterfly. "Isn't he beautiful?"

"Very." Gold paused. "Where's the other one?"

"I imagine he'll be along any moment," she said.

He looked down the track and saw a dark, muscular colt prance onto the dirt, his powerful body lathered with sweat, his groom frantically holding on to his bridle in an attempt to stop him from running off.

"It's not going to be much of a race," remarked Plaga. "That animal is having a nervous breakdown."

The dark horse shook his head, failing to dislodge the groom, then spun in a tight circle, lifting the groom completely off the ground while the jockey clung helplessly to his neck.

The announcer spoke up again. "Stepping onto the track in the cerise and white diamonds of the Seballa Cartel is Seattle Slew." He went on to recite the colt's record, pointing out that due to a record-keeping error he had merely been named Seattle during his two most recent incarnations. The current version, he informed the crowd, had just turned four years old the previous week. The experts, he concluded, still hadn't decided whether he was officially black or dark brown, the distinction having something to do with the color of the hairs on his nostrils.

Suddenly Gold was aware of Titania standing in front of him, whistling melodically and making a number of graceful but incomprehensible gestures with her hands.

The Steel Butterfly asked her to repeat what she had done, then nodded, and Titania headed back to her seat.

"What was *that* all about?" asked Gold.

"I *think* she just bet me two hundred credits that the black horse beats my red one," said the Steel Butterfly. "I suppose I'll find out for sure once she picks up her translating device."

Gold watched the little alien's retreating form. "Prostitution *and* gambling? The *Comet* seems to specialize in corrupting innocence, be it mechanical or alien."

"It's only fair," replied the Steel Butterfly amiably. "She's certainly corrupted enough of our patrons."

"Disgusting," muttered Gold.

"But pretty," added the Steel Butterfly as Gold continued to watch the petite faerie.

Flustered, he self-consciously turned his attention back to the horses, which were cantering up and down the track as the announcer explained that this was not the race itself, but merely a brief warming-up process.

"Which one do you like, Doctor Gold?" asked Fiona Bradley, leaning forward from her position directly behind him.

"I have no opinion."

"All for the best, I suppose," she replied. "I've

never been to a horserace, but I imagine the trophy presenter should be impartial."

"Which one do *you* like?" asked Plaga.

"Oh, the red one," said the gray-haired executive. "He's absolutely gorgeous."

"They both look pretty much alike to me," said Gold.

"Surely you can't mean that," interjected Plaga. "The black one looks like he's going to start foaming at the mouth any second."

"Perhaps he's just anxious to run," said Gold.

"With that lather all over him?" said Plaga smugly. "He's already burned up more energy than he'll use in the race."

"If you say so."

"You think otherwise?" persisted Plaga.

"I don't know anything about horseracing."

"Then perhaps you'd like to make a small wager, so you'll have a rooting interest."

"No, thank you," said Gold. "And I already have a rooting interest."

"Oh? Which one?"

"The one you're all rooting against, of course."

"Would you care to put one hundred credits on that?"

"I don't believe in gambling."

"Not even a small friendly bet?" urged Plaga.

"You are not my friend."

Plaga glanced questioningly at Fiona Bradley, but her attention seemed focused on the two horses. "Well," he said condescendingly, "if you haven't the courage of your convictions . . ."

"I have always had the courage of my convictions," said Gold. "That's why you invited me up here, in case it's slipped your mind."

"Then why not just admit the red horse looks better to you?"

"He doesn't."

"Of course not," said Plaga with heavy sarcasm.

"Are you calling me a liar?"

"Certainly not," said Plaga with false assurance. "If you don't want to bet with me, there's no law that says you have to."

"Mr. Plaga, my religion doesn't allow me to wager," said Gold coldly. "On the other hand, it also instructs me to puncture pomposity and hypocrisy wherever I may find it. You know no more about horseracing than I do, and you have been trying to goad me into entering a contract that is contrary to my convictions. Therefore, since I must either enter a transaction or back down before my enemy, I agree to invest one credit on the black horse."

"Only one?" laughed Plaga.

"Is it the transaction that is important to you, or the amount?"

Plaga grinned. "Doctor Gold, you've got yourself a bet."

"No," said Gold. "Betting implies the element of chance. I have an investment."

"You seem awfully confident," interjected the Steel Butterfly.

"The Lord is my shepherd. He won't let me lose."

"Not even one credit?" she asked with an amused smile.

"Not even one credit," he replied with conviction.

"How comforting to know that God is on your side," said Plaga.

"God isn't on *my* side; I'm on *His*."

"A subtle distinction."

"Not to Him, it isn't," replied Gold.

"Shall we let the Steel Butterfly hold the stakes until the race is over?" suggested Plaga.

Gold looked directly into Plaga's eyes. "You'll forgive me if I refuse your offer, but I have no doubt that you still have a number of cameras trained on me, and I wouldn't want anyone to think that I was concluding one of the *Velvet Comet*'s more mundane business transactions."

The executive flashed him an unembarrassed smile, and turned his attention back to the track.

At last the two colts had begun approaching the starting gate, and the crowd quickly became silent, finally interested in the proceedings.

"I should have given you odds," chuckled Plaga, as Seattle Slew reared up behind the gate.

Gold made no comment.

The announcer concluded his prerace commentary by listing all the various mile-and-a-quarter records, qualifying them by world, gravity, oxygen content in the air, and weight carried by each horse.

The two colts walked into the gate. As instant later a bell rang, the doors flew open, and Seattle Slew quickly assumed a commanding lead.

"Possibly I should have given *you* odds," remarked Gold.

"They've got a long way to run yet," said Plaga confidently.

The black colt in the lead seemed to be continually demanding more rein from his jockey, as if there were nothing in his life that he cherished more than piercing a hole in the wind. The chestnut, after the initial few seconds, fell into stride behind the leader, loping along with no apparent effort.

"Exciting, isn't it?" asked the Steel Butterfly.

Gold made no reply.

As the two colts passed the halfway point in the race, Secretariat's jockey tapped him once with the whip, and the chestnut colt surged forward. His long strides quickly ate into the margin between himself and the free-running leader, and he pulled to within half a length of the burly black colt.

"Here he comes!" cried the Steel Butterfly, as the members of the crowd started screaming the names of the horses.

Seattle Slew's jockey asked his horse to respond, and the black colt shot forward, finally freed of all restraint, and opened the lead to a length once again, his flying hooves beating a rhythmic tattoo on the dirt flooring. Twice more during the final two hundred yards Secretariat pulled to within almost even terms; twice more Seattle Slew dug in and refused to let his rival go by. As they thundered past the grandstand and the finish line, necks extended, muscles straining, the lathered black colt still clung tenaciously to his narrow lead.

"Shit!" muttered Plaga disgustedly.

"Well, Doctor Gold, I guess Gustave owes you a credit," said the Steel Butterfly, exhilarated by the contest she had just witnessed despite the defeat of her horse. She noticed that Gold was staring intently at a spot near the rail some forty yards before the finish line.

"Doctor Gold?" she repeated, touching him gently on the shoulder.

He straightened up abruptly. "Yes?"

"What did you think of it?"

"The race?" he asked.

"Of course."

"Very exciting," he said unenthusiastically.

"Come along, Doctor Gold," said Fiona Bradley, starting to climb down from the grandstand.

"I beg your pardon?"

"You have to present the trophy."

He nodded absently and followed her up to the presentation platform, where they were joined by the other division heads. The black horse was still a quarter of a mile away, jogging slowly back toward the grandstand, and Gold's attention wandered back to the same spot on the rail.

"You seem pensive, Doctor Gold," said Fiona Bradley after a moment.

"You'd think they would have wings," he murmured wistfully.

"Well, they certainly ran as if they did," she replied.

He stared at her, surprised, for a moment, then quickly regained his composure.

"Didn't they, though?" he agreed at last.

3

Fiona Bradley sipped her coffee and admired the view from her new apartment. Deluros VIII could be a pretty overwhelming world from ground level, but from up here on the 142nd story of the Vainmill Building, there was a certain delicate beauty to the thousands of towers and spires that pierced the blue sky.

The planet itself was the soon-to-be capital of the race of Man. No one knew quite when the government would officially abandon Earth for Deluros VIII, but for all practical purposes the transition had already taken place. The planet had ten times the surface area of Man's birth-place, and was, galactically speaking, much more in the center of things. The planet's single city—which, strangely, had never been given a name—covered every square inch of surface area, snaking through deserts and even connecting the three major continents by means of vast enclosed underwater thoroughfares.

Fiona gazed out through the wall of windows,

enjoying the view from the top, figuratively and literally. Both were new to her, but she had been preparing herself for them for years.

Finally she turned her attention back to the business at hand, and activated her personal computer.

"I'm going down to eighty-six now," she announced. "Hold all messages."

"Registered," replied the computer.

"Is Gustave Plaga there yet?"

"Checking . . . yes."

"Good," she said grimly.

"Will there be anything else?" asked the computer.

"Not right now." She paused. "Yes. Get in touch with Miranda Torres and tell her that the interior decorator she hired is unacceptable."

"Would you like her to hire another?"

"I'll pick my own."

She walked to her private elevator, waited for the doors to dilate, and stepped into the compartment.

"Eighty-six," she commanded, then turned to look out of the glass enclosure as it began its descent, wondering why tradition had it that the chairman of Vainmill always directed the immense corporation's affairs from the eighty-sixth floor, and deciding that once her apartment had finally been decorated to her tastes it would be time to make a break with that particular tradition. "We have arrived," announced the elevator.

Fiona waited for the doors to dilate again, then walked out into a large, elegantly furnished office. Gustave Plaga, who had been waiting nervously for her, got to his feet and remained standing while she walked across the plush carpet and seated herself behind the polished desk that had served some twenty-six previous Vainmill chairmen, each of whom stared severely out at Plaga from holographs on the walls.

"Please sit down, Gustave," said Fiona.

Plaga sat down on a hard, uncomfortable chair, crossed his legs, and tried unsuccessfully to assume an air of nonchalance. Fiona, sitting in her own chair, swiveled slightly in order to face him directly.

"Gustave," she said at last. "I must strike you as a very stupid woman."

Plaga made no reply, but shifted nervously in his chair.

"Did you really think I wouldn't find out what you had done?"

"I'm not quite sure I know what you're talking about," said Plaga.

She stared at him for a long moment, while he tried to meet her eyes and shifted uncomfortably.

"You have almost single-handedly turned a minor irritant into a major disaster," she said. "You *are* aware of that, aren't you?"

Plaga opened his mouth to protest, then thought better of it and remained silent.

"I did not spend two-thirds of my life reaching the chairmanship of Vainmill, only to preside over its dissolution. Is that perfectly clear?"

"You don't know all the facts," he protested.

"Is that perfectly clear?" she repeated harshly.

"Perfectly," said Plaga.

"Thomas Gold was the reason for my predecessor's downfall," she continued. "He will not be the reason for mine." She looked directly at Plaga. "Just how long did you think you could keep this secret from me, Gustave?"

"It was never intended to be a secret," said Plaga defensively.

"Surely you didn't think you could keep it from the press?"

"I hadn't considered it."

"Then why did you do it at all?"

"Executives are supposed to act on their own initiative," said Plaga petulantly. "That's just what I did."

"And you saw absolutely no downside risk in arresting the entire Jesus Pure population of Delvania?"

"You make it sound enormous," said Plaga. "There are only twenty-seven of them—and one of them is guilty of stealing Vainmill property."

"Gustave, you're a fool," she said coldly. "Two days ago we had one irritating preacher whose capacity to harm Vainmill or the *Comet* was negligible. Today we have twenty-seven martyrs. There is nothing any of them could have done that would justify their incarceration."

"You don't *know* what they did," complained Plaga.

"Of course I know what they did!" she snapped. "Do you think the chairman of Vainmill is without her own sources of information?"

"Then you know why I had them arrested."

"There was never any doubt in my mind why you had them arrested," said Fiona. "You were guilty of a catastrophic error in judgment."

"Surely you don't propose that we simply turn a blind eye to the fact that one of our computers had been robbed!"

"*Anything* would have been better than your particular reaction," said Fiona. She activated her desktop intercom. "Coffee."

She waited for a secretary to enter the office with two cups of black coffee.

"Will you join me?" asked Fiona.

"No, thank you," said Plaga.

Fiona shrugged, waited for her coffee, took a sip of it, and then turned her attention back to Plaga as the secretary left.

"Gustave, I've been listening to you and the rest of Vainmill's executives talk about Gold for the past five years, and I must confess that I've never seen a problem handled so badly from start to finish. You still don't know what kind of man you're up against."

"He's a religious fanatic," said Plaga.

"That's too simplistic an answer. Thomas Gold is an obsessive personality. He truly believes that his actions all stem from the purest of motives, and that he has a private pipeline straight from God's lips to his ear. He's also a man with a temper, who can always find some means of justifying his actions, no matter how out of character they may seem. That's why I didn't stop you from goading him into making that bet with you—I wanted to see how much abuse he was willing to take, and once he passed that point I wanted to see how he matched his actions against his beliefs. It should have been apparent to you from that one incident alone that this is a man who will find a way to rationalize anything he feels he must do to obtain his goals, and yet you continue to make the mistake of thinking that he can be placated, that closing down a mine on Belargo IV or donating ten million credits to his church or setting up an Alien Education Fund on Pollux IV will satisfy him and make him turn his attentions elsewhere. And, predictably, he has taken every such gesture as a sign of weakness. You can't reach an accommodation with a man like this; you have to fight him."

'That's just what I was trying to do!" said Plaga in frustration.

"All right," said Fiona. "You fought him. Now suppose you tell me what you think you accomplished."

"It was a reprisal," said Plaga sullenly.

"And just what did you think a reprisal would do?" demanded Fiona. "Has it harmed Gold in any way? Has it helped us? All you've done is given him new fuel for his fire, and forced me to humiliate myself and Vainmill by publicly apologizing to him."

"But they broke into our computer on Delvania!" persisted Plaga.

"It was broken into," she agreed, "but almost certainly not by any of the people you had arrested. If you had examined their dossiers, as I did, you'd know that none of them had the necessary skill to pull off a job like that."

"Even if you're right," said Plaga, "it seems likely that they commissioned the job. I thought we might get to them before they had a chance to pass the information on to Gold."

"That's the stupidest thing you've said yet!" she exploded. "Gold or one of his representatives had what they needed ten minutes after the theft. You didn't authorize any arrests for twelve hours."

"I was trying to save the *Comet*," repeated Plaga stubbornly.

"You haven't heard a word I've said, have you? Gold doesn't give a damn about the *Velvet Comet*! It's Vainmill he's after."

"The stuff he stole can only be used against the *Comet*," persisted Plaga.

Fiona sighed wearily. "How can you be so foolish when you're trying to be so clever, Gustave? If he just wanted to close down the *Comet*, he'd lobby to make prostitution illegal in the Deluros system, he'd preach more about the immorality of sex without marriage, and if he got desperate enough, he'd find a way to plant a bomb up there. But look at what he stole: holographic records of the faeries' training sessions at Suma's school, and copies of their contracts. He wants to destroy Vainmill because of our exploitation of alien races; the *Velvet Comet* is just a temporary battlefield. In fact, he expects us to close it down in exchange for his moderating his attacks against us."

She finished her coffee, then continued: "Thomas Gold himself is a mild irritant—or at least he was until you decided to make Vainmill policy. The holographic footage he's got will be an embarrassment, though if he uses it unwisely it will probably do us as much good as harm, people being what they are. But irritants and embarrassments are one thing, and disasters are another. Arresting the entire Jesus Pure population of Delvania is a disaster."

"Then I suppose we'd better set them free," said Plaga grudgingly.

"I gave the order six hours ago. Vainmill has also agreed to pay each of them half a million credits as full settlement for any grievances they may have over their treatment."

"That's blackmail!" protested Plaga.

"It's pragmatism," she replied. "I had our attorney offer them the money *before* they thought of making any demands, in exchange for their writ-

ten agreement not to make any in the future." She
paused. "My next step, after I leave this office,
will be to go down to our holo studio on the
forty-third floor and tape a public apology for
Vainmill's actions."

"Do you think that's wise?" asked Plaga.

"I think it's essential," answered Fiona. She stared
meaningfully at him. "I also intend to state that
the man responsible for this regrettable incident
has been fired."

"That's not fair!" said Plaga.

"Was it fair of you to arrest twenty-seven innocent people?" asked Fiona. "Or to usurp my authority less than a week after I'd been elected
chairman?"

"But, damn it, I did it in the best interests of
Vainmill!"

"I know," answered Fiona calmly. "That's why
I'm firing you."

"I don't understand," said Plaga.

"If you had been trying some power play to
take the company away from me before I'd learned
my way around the job, it would be understandable. Not forgivable, but understandable. And if I
thought you were doing this just to impress me
with your initiative, even *that* would be understandable, though, of course, I would have had to
let you go anyway. But I truly believe that you
thought you were doing something beneficial to
Vainmill, and such incredibly poor judgment is
perhaps the worst sin an executive can commit: it
cannot go unpunished. And our little conversation has convinced me that you would be guilty of
any number of equally embarrassing and ill-
conceived blunders if I allowed you to remain
with the company."

"And what about you?" demanded Plaga hotly.

"I am responsible to our Board of Directors, and I am exercising such damage control as I can before they ask for my resignation as well." She paused. "I believe that concludes our business, Gustave. Your accrued profit-sharing has been deposited in your personal account, and I have instructed the comptroller to pay you through noon today. I realize that a generous severance settlement is customary in such cases, but frankly, you don't deserve it."

"I'll sue for it," threatened Plaga.

"That's your privilege," replied Fiona. "You know how to get in touch with our legal department." She checked her timepiece. "And now, if you will excuse me, I have a considerable amount of work to do, most of it caused by you."

She stared emotionlessly at him until he finally rose and walked to the door.

"This isn't over yet!" Plaga promised.

"It was over, Gustave, the day that you came to the erroneous conclusion that Thomas Gold thought like you, and could be bought or bullied like you."

He muttered something that she couldn't quite hear and stalked out the door.

She swiveled in her chair and looked out the window. This one didn't afford her the view that she had from her apartment. From the eighty-sixth floor, the city seemed to be nothing but an enormous expanse of nearly identical office buildings, many of which flew their company colors from scores of flagpoles. She preferred the view from the 142nd, where the glass towers resembled stately minarets of ancient days. Still, the eighty-sixth was where the ultimate power of Vainmill was concentrated, and it was from here that she would exercise it, at least until she finished converting her apartment. With a sigh, she turned back to her desk and activated an intercom.

"All right," she said. "You can come in now."

A moment later Richard Constantine entered the office and walked directly to a chair. He was a rotund, balding, conservatively dressed man in his early thirties, who seemed totally unprepossessing until one looked into his shrewd, metallic eyes.

"I assume you saw the whole thing on your monitor?" asked Fiona.

He nodded. "Yes."

"Good. That saves me the trouble of recounting it." She looked across her desk at Constantine. "You've probably guessed why you're here?"

"You want me to take over the Entertainment and Leisure Division," he replied with conviction.

Fiona nodded. "That's correct. I must say that you don't look very happy about it, Richard."

"Nobody's very happy when he's presented with a ticking bomb—even one that's been gift-wrapped." He leaned back on his chair. "Entertainment and Leisure makes less money than any of the other divisions, and it has ten times the problems—and that's *without* Tom Gold taking potshots at it."

"It's only temporary," she explained. "Just long enough to get things straightened out."

"You're sure?" he said dubiously. "The attrition rate for Entertainment and Leisure presidents isn't exactly a secret."

"Richard, you're my most trusted assistant. I have no intention of marooning you in Entertainment and Leisure. I need you too much right here."

"Then why not give it to someone else?"

"Because, as you said, it's a ticking bomb. I want to make sure it's properly dismantled."

"Let me get this straight," he said. "Are you referring to the division or to Tom Gold?"

"To the division, of course," replied Fiona. "As annoying as Thomas Gold is, he's far from Entertainment and Leisure's only problem. Our hotel chain in the Quinellus cluster is losing an enormous amount of money, two of our video networks have been mismanaged almost into bankruptcy, our health spas are down thirty percent this year—and, of course, there's no telling how many of his underlings share Gustave's unique approach to problem-solving. As for the division itself, I have no intention of dismantling it; if I did, I would have given it to Mildred Nambuta. *Her* job is killing companies that I don't want to be bothered with; *yours* is saving them."

"How long will I be there?" asked Constantine.

"Until the job is done," she answered. "I want to totally reorganize Vainmill, to make the various divisions less autonomous than they've been in the past. I want you to attack the major problems in Entertainment and Leisure, get rid of the deadwood, and when everything is in place I also want you to suggest a permanent successor. I would guess you'll have everything in order within a year—and I will be seriously displeased if it takes more than a year and a half."

"And then?" he asked, staring directly at her.

"And then, if you've done a good job, there will be rewards."

"Well," he said, relaxing, "you've never lied to me yet."

"I was wondering when you'd get around to

remembering that," said Fiona. "Now try to look a little happier."

"I wasn't aware that looking happy was a job requirement," he said sardonically.

She smiled at him. "From your expression, one would think I was sending you off to manage some theater on the Outer Frontier. Really, Richard, you should be flattered that I trust you to take charge of the situation."

"I'd be even more flattered if you gave me Acquisitions or Finance," he said, returning her smile.

"You'd be wasted there. You're my troubleshooter, so it's only natural that I should send you to the most troublesome division we have." She paused. "I'll have to get the Board's approval to make it official—but I hardly think they're likely to refuse my request a week after electing me."

Her intercom beeped twice.

"Yes, Marina?" she said, as the hologram of her personal secretary appeared a foot above the desktop.

"I've contacted Yakim Keno, as you requested," said the dark-haired woman, "and he has agreed to direct you. He's waiting in the studio right now."

"Good."

"I've also taken the liberty of sending for your makeup artist. Oh, and I've told Nina Reid that we'll want to release copies of the tape to the media by midafternoon."

"Excellent. Tell them I'll be down there in a few minutes."

"Will you be giving any live interviews afterward?"

"No, I don't think so. We'll let the statement stand alone, and hope some bank theft or murder knocks us out of the headlines."

"Very good," said the secretary, breaking the connection.

"Speaking of your statement, have you any particular advice concerning our friend Gold?" asked Constantine.

"What do *you* think we should do, Richard?" she asked.

"Nothing," he replied promptly.

"Absolutely nothing?"

He nodded. "Sometimes nothing is the very best thing to do." He paused. "There's no sense demanding the holos back; he'll never return them, and we don't want him to think they're that important to us. Also, if we attack him for stealing them, we'd make him look like some kind of hero."

"I quite agree." She smiled. "You know, you really *are* the right man for the job, Richard."

"I never said I wasn't. I'd just rather work *here*, where the power is."

"You'll find there's sufficient power to be wielded as acting president of Entertainment and Leisure," she assured him. "Including the power to ignore an annoyance like Thomas Gold."

"Then that's our official policy?"

"From this day forward," she agreed. "No matter what Gold demands, we won't decommission the *Comet*, nor will we offer any other concessions to him. Vainmill has made its last attempt to bribe him or otherwise purchase his goodwill or benign neglect. Thomas Gold is an unyielding man, and we will therefore indulge in no more ill-fated attempts to make him yield." She paused and leaned forward over her desk. "Once I tape my apology, he is a nonperson. If anyone asks our opinion of him, we think he's an honorable man with whom we have an honorable disagreement. Also, we en-

joyed his company on the *Velvet Comet* and hope to
meet him there again in the future. If no one
asks, we won't even volunteer that much."

"Let's hope it's that easy," said Constantine.

"It will be—at least for *me*. There's a miners'
strike on Praesape II that's costing us tens of millions of credits per day, we're being sued by the
Seballa Cartel over a number of tachyon-drive
patents, there's been a military takeover on Bow-
man XXIII that's frozen a considerable portion of
our assets in their banking system, and besides all
that, I'm still learning my job." She smiled. "Yes, I
think I won't have all that much difficulty ignoring Thomas Gold. It may be a little harder for *you*,
but that's what I'm paying you for."

"I don't know exactly what was on those holos
that he swiped. Once they're released, how much
damage can they do us?"

"I haven't seen them either," admitted Fiona. "I
gather they're quite pornographic, and that there
are hours of them. They might do us some
damage—but nothing fatal, I assure you. It took
three hundred years to build the Vainmill Syndicate into what it has become; no one man is going
to bring it down. Vainmill will still be going strong
after you and I and Thomas Gold have all re-
verted to dust."

"I suppose there's always a chance that the holos
will backfire on him, too," commented Constantine thoughtfully. "Deluros is a pretty sophisticated world. He might bring us in more business
than he scares away."

"Perhaps," said Fiona dubiously. She paused. "I
can't tell you how much I dislike the notion of
those little aliens being the center of this contro-
versy. I would never expect Doctor Gold to be-

lieve it, but I find Vainmill's historical treatment of aliens as distasteful as he does."

"Your feelings about the subject notwithstanding," said Constantine carefully, "I don't see how we can get rid of the faeries for the foreseeable future. It would seem as if we were caving in to him."

"I know," she said, her face set and hard. "Thomas Gold isn't the only person who can't be bought or intimidated. Whatever I decide to do about Vainmill's exploitation of aliens in the future, it won't be because of any pressure that he tries to bring to bear on the issue." She paused. "In fact, that was the very first problem I had hoped to attack as chairman—and though Thomas Gold will never believe it, he and he alone is the reason that I've put the project on an indefinite hold." She glanced at her timepiece. "Speaking of the estimable Doctor Gold, I see that I'm already overdue at the studio." She got to her feet. "As soon as I'm through down there, I'll inform the necessary parties that you are the acting president of Entertainment and Leisure."

"Then I guess I'd better get started on my homework," said Constantine. He looked thoughtful. "I'll give Plaga the rest of the day to clean out his office before I move in, which means it might be a little awkward to start tapping his computer files until Security gets a chance to change the Priority Code on them." He paused. "I suppose I can start going over whatever we've got on Gold. We may be officially ignoring him, but as long as he's not likely to return the favor I ought to learn everything I can about him."

"A good idea," she agreed, walking to the elevator.

"He's got to have a weakness *some*where."

"Most men do," said Fiona, commanding the doors to open. "Even a moral man like Thomas Gold."

"I like moral men the best."

"Oh?" she said, stepping into the elevator. "Why is that?"

Constantine smiled. "They always make the loudest crash when they fall."

4

Christina Gilbert looked up from the newstape she had been viewing and saw her father and her five-year-old son enter the small apartment, hand in hand.

"Hi," she said. "You look exhausted."

Gold walked over to an easy chair and plopped down on it.

"I am," he replied. "I must be getting old."

"You're late," she noted. "We were starting to worry about you."

"There were a number of new exhibits," explained Gold. "They've even added a pair of tigers from Earth itself." He watched with a weary smile as his grandson began enthusiastically reciting all the wonders he had seen.

Christina listened to her child for a moment while Gold put his feet up on a hassock, then sent the boy off to wash his hands and change his clothes.

"He seems to have had a good time," she said when he had left the room.

"We both did," replied Gold. "The zoo is a wonderful place to take children."

"I always suspected it might be," she replied with a smile.

Gold sighed. "I know. I wish I had had more time to spend with you and your brother when you were growing up, but I felt called upon to do the Lord's work."

"You still do."

He nodded. "But age and gravity catch up with all of us sooner or later. I've slowed down."

"I wonder if the Vainmill people think so," she said with an amused smile.

"They're the enemy," he replied. "They get my adrenaline flowing. I'm like an athlete who's nearing the end of his career: I can get up for the big games, but I coast too much of the time." He paused, an ironic expression on his face. "Still, even coasting can find some favor in the eyes of the Lord. More than halfway through my life I've discovered the joy of being a grandfather."

Christina laughed aloud and shifted her position on the well-worn sofa. "I'd say you're coasting about as much as that Seattle horse did last week."

"What do you know about that?" asked Gold, surprised.

"The holos of the race were broadcast on all the networks," she answered. "I gather that it was the sporting highlight of the month, except for a couple of prizefights."

"Even out in the Albion Cluster?"

She nodded. "We're not quite the uninformed rustics that my brother seems to think we are."

"Did they show the trophy presentation?" asked Gold.

Christina nodded. "In all its glory." She paused. "Fiona Bradley doesn't look all that formidable."

"She won't be after this Friday," predicted Gold confidently.

"The madam looks like an interesting lady, though," she continued in a bantering tone.

"She isn't. She's just a businesswoman who doesn't seem to realize that she's working for Satan."

"Anyway, it was an exciting race. I think I could become a fan." She smiled mischievously. "Simon tells me that you won a bet on it. He sounded very disapproving."

"Your brother talks too much," said Gold. "It was done to put a rather nasty man in his place, and I've apologized to God for it." Gold grimaced. "But sometimes Simon is a little less forgiving than the Lord."

"Only sometimes?" she said sardonically. "He must be improving."

Gold chuckled. "What can I say? I wanted a godly son to carry on my work. I got one."

She shook her head. "*You're* godly. Simon's just a pompous ass."

"You're wrong," said Gold, suddenly serious. "He's a better Christian than I am. If I seemed critical of him, it's the sin of envy; I compare myself with him and wish I had his dedication."

"Well, *I* compare him with you, and wish he had your humanity," responded his daughter earnestly.

"If Fiona Bradley could hear you say that, she'd probably put a hit out on him."

"Vainmill doesn't actually hire assassins, does it?"

"Vainmill does whatever Vainmill thinks is necessary, whether it's eradicating entire alien civilizations or bribing government officials or rigging elections." He noticed her sudden concern. "There's no need to worry," he said reassuringly. "Your brother is one of our best-kept secrets; I doubt that Vainmill even knows he exists."

"I wasn't worried about Simon."

"Don't worry about me, either," said Gold. "I don't plan to die while I have so much of the Lord's work left to do—and if God *should* happen to decree my death, I guarantee that it won't be at the hands of Fiona Bradley and her underlings."

"I hope you're right."

"I know I am." he paused. "By the way, where's your mother?"

"In the kitchen, getting up her courage," said Christina.

"Why?"

"While you were at the zoo with Jeremy, I spent the afternoon styling her hair, and now she's afraid you won't like it."

"What difference does it make?" asked Gold. "Like it or not, I gather I'm stuck with it."

"It matters to *her*."

"Well, bring her in here and let's get it over with," said Gold.

"Tell her you like it," said Christina.

"If I do, I will."

Christina seemed about to say something else, changed her mind, and walked down a short corridor to the kitchen. She returned a moment later with her mother in tow.

Corinne Gold was fifty-four years old, and the gravity that her husband had complained about was more apparent on her. Gold thought of her as sturdy, but in truth she was fat. A number of crooked teeth which had gone uncorrected during her youth gave her lips a pursed, thoughtful look.

She wore no jewelry, as befitted the wife of the leader of the Jesus Pures, and no attempt had been made to fight back the rush of gray that had spread through her hair. But she was friendly, and pious, and devoted to her husband and his work. And, for the moment, she was *very* nervous.

Gold stared at her for a long moment, trying to get used to the wave in the front.

"Well?" said Corinne anxiously. "What do you think?"

"It's very becoming," he lied.

"Then you're not upset?"

"Of course not. But it will take me a while to get used to seeing you like this."

"That's because you're conservative," said Corinne, visibly relieved.

"Of course I am," replied Gold. "The whole purpose of my life has been to conserve what is good and eradicate what isn't."

"Well, that's *one* definition," said Corinne. She turned to her daughter. "You know, he still gets upset whenever I rearrange the furniture. I can't even move the holos on the walls."

"And is everybody still forbidden to straighten up the mess on his desk?" asked Christina.

"Absolutely," answered Corinne. She smiled at Gold. "That's conservatism for you."

Gold's grandson, freshly scrubbed, entered the room and held out his hands for Christina to inspect them.

"When's dinner?" he asked.

"As soon as your Uncle Simon arrives," replied Corinne.

"How about Daddy?" asked Jeremy.

"He's working tonight," said Christina.

"Again?" said Gold. "I do believe he's going to

make it through the entire two weeks of your visit without once seeing Simon."

"Just talented, I guess," said Christina.

"It really is for the best, Thomas," added Corinne. "You know they'd just spend the night arguing."

"One of these days I'm going to have to get the pair of them together and shake them each by the scruff of the neck until they agree to behave like reasonable adults."

"The time to shake Simon by the scruff of the neck was twenty-five years ago," said Christina dryly. "I think you might find it a bit difficult these days."

"I think I'll go set the table," said Corinne, who had long since realized that her children didn't like each other, but still didn't care to hear them talk about it. "Would you like to help me, Jeremy? You can tell me all about the zoo."

The boy shook his head.

"I really think your grandmother needs your help," suggested Gold gently.

"I'm tired," said Jeremy, forcing himself to yawn and stretch.

"Well, if you're *that* tired, maybe we'd better stay home tomorrow instead of going to the aquarium. . . ." He watched while Jeremy considered this statement, and then walked over to stand beside his grandmother. "I guess you're not as tired as you thought."

"I guess not," agreed Jeremy, following Corinne into the dining room.

"Last night his leg was too sore, if I recall correctly," commented Gold with a smile. "At least he's creative."

"You know, if Simon or I had ever pulled that

routine on you, we'd have gotten a ten-minute lecture about lying, followed by a sound thrashing," noted Christina.

"I save my lectures and my thrashings for my enemies these days," responded Gold. "Besides, he's only five years old."

"I don't remember that being five ever got us any special dispensation when you were raising us."

Gold smiled. "That's because children are for raising; grandchildren are for spoiling."

"Well, you're doing your best," she laughed.

"Acutally," said Gold with a sigh, "when we're not looking at animals or entertainers or athletes, I seem to spend most of my time explaining why his religion forbids his eating all the things he wants me to buy for him." He frowned. "There are more than two million Jesus Pures on Deluros; you'd think the concession stands would take that into account."

"They will, when there's enough of a demand," replied Christina. "Don't forget: most of your followers would sooner read the Bible than look at captive animals."

"Most of them don't have five-year-old grandsons," said Gold defensively. "I've never said that our lives have to be joyless, just moral."

"Well, now that they've seen holos of you sitting next to the Iron Moth, or whatever she calls herself, maybe they'll start believing you."

"The Steel Butterfly," he said wryly. "I wish I knew how they decide upon their names up there. Do you know what the Chief of Security is named?"

"What?"

"Attila! And one of the prostitutes was named Perfumed Garden."

"I wonder what it represents?" mused Christina.

"I hope I never find out," answered Gold. "You know, even the computer has a name."

"Really? What is it?"

"Cupid, of all things."

She looked at him for a moment, as if weighing her next statement.

"What *was* it like up there on the *Velvet Comet*?" she asked at last.

He frowned. "Why?"

"Just curiosity," she replied. "Hadn't you ever wondered before you got there?"

"Never once."

"Well, I guess I'm just not as moral as you," she said with a smile. "I'm absolutely fascinated."

Gold stared at her. "Every now and then, when I least expect it, I find myself agreeing with Simon," he said wryly. "I think Robert may be a bad influence upon you."

She returned his stare with no trace of uneasiness or embarrassment. "I was curious about houses of ill repute long before I married Bob. It's perfectly natural. Now why don't you tell me all about it?" she coaxed him.

"There's very little to tell," said Gold. "I imagine you've seen advertisements for it."

"You're not getting off the hook *that* easily." She grinned. "Come on, now—what's it *really* like?"

"Seriously?"

"Seriously."

"All right, " said Gold. "I went up there expecting to find Satan, and I did. What I had forgotten was that he is a fallen angel."

"I don't think I follow you," said Christina.

"I mean that everything that happens up there is moral under certain circumstances. The pleasures of the flesh are acceptable, even desirable, within the confines of marriage. And it's hardly sinful to eat or shop or be entertained or to work out in a gymnasium or to watch a sporting event. But there comes a point when eating becomes gluttony, and seeking constant entertainment becomes sloth, and spending money on expensive presents becomes excessive and wasteful. It's a blurred line, and different for every man and woman, and as a result values get very confused up there. They make sin very comfortable."

"I suppose people wouldn't sin if it weren't comfortable, so to speak," offered Christina.

"They make it *too* attractive," said Gold. "You asked about their names before. I suspect they all take such names because it lends to the illusion they're trying to create." He paused. "Don't forget: it isn't God who is known as the Prince of Liars."

"Are half of the prostitutes really men?"

"All but two are Men."

Christina smiled. "I meant the gender, not the species."

"I have no idea." He glanced sharply at her. "I trust that *you* have no idea, either."

"What about the two aliens?" asked Christina. "Do humans actually go to bed with them?"

"So I am told," said Gold, suddenly uneasy. "I find the subject distasteful in the extreme."

"I saw a holo of them after your sermon last Friday," persisted Christina. "Do they really look like that?"

"I don't know what they looked like in the holo," answered Gold.

"Like little pixies, with pointed ears and oversized blue eyes."

"Something like that."

"Is that silver hair they have, or is it feathers?"

"How should I know?" he snapped. "I'm not one of their customers!"

"Don't be so touchy," she said, ignoring his outburst. "I'm just curious about them."

"Then tie in to the main library computer and ask for data on the Andrican race of Besmarith II. You'll find out everything you want to know."

"I'm not *that* curious," replied Christina. "I just thought you might give me some details."

"The subject is closed," he said. "I am not going to discuss or describe a pair of alien prostitutes for your amusement."

"I resent that!"

He scrutinized her for a moment.

"Then I apologize," he said. "It's just that I can't help feeling that I'm adding to their exploitation by talking about them in this manner."

"Accepted, as always," she said, walking over and kissing him on the cheek.

"Friends again?" asked Gold.

She smiled. "If I can ask another question."

"About the *Comet* or the faeries?"

"The Steel Butterfly."

He nodded. "Go ahead."

"What makes her do what she does?"

"What makes any sinner sin?" responded Gold.

"But she looked so elegant and sounded so sophisticated, at least from what little they showed of her. Surely there are other things she could do for a living."

"Not all sinners are inelegant and unsophisticated," said Gold. "In fact, quite the contrary: a sophisticated man can come up with one hundred well-reasoned humanistic rationalizations for assuaging his hungers at the expense of his soul; the simple man is usually better able to differentiate right from wrong and act accordingly. As for the Steel Butterfly, she doesn't think that being the madam of a brothel is sinful. She views making money as an honorable enterprise, and doubtless views her sexual technique as an art form. Which," he added, "is the problem with rationalizations: they work beautifully on Men, but God is not impressed by them. Good and Evil *do* exist, and all the rationalization in the world will not turn an immoral act into a moral one."

"You're preaching again," said Christina, amused.

"It's what I do," responded Gold. "It's what I am."

The front door's computer lock clicked open, and Simon Gold entered the apartment. He was tall, even taller than Gold, and far more muscular. Everything about him seemed somehow severe: the cut of his clothes, the style of his hair, the expression on his face.

"Good afternoon, sister," he said formally.

"Hello, Simon," answered Christina. "We've been waiting for you."

"Including your husband?"

"No. Bob's busy again tonight. He sends his apologies."

He stared emotionlessly at her for a moment, then turned to Gold.

"You look tired, Father," he said.

"I'm not as young as I used to be," said Gold. "Or else the zoo is a lot bigger than *it* used to be. Probably both."

"Possibly you should let the boy's father take him to the zoo while you concentrate on more important things," suggested Simon with no show of sympathy.

"I think not," said Gold. "Twenty-five years from now Robert can take *his* grandchild to the zoo."

"Doubtless," replied Simon.

"How was *your* day?" inquired Gold.

"Satisfactory."

"Did you get any more research done on your book?"

"Some."

"I didn't know you were writing a book," said Christina.

"I'm not," replied Simon. "I'm *researching* a book. I won't begin writing it until sometime next spring. I expect it to take about three years."

"What's it about?" she asked.

He merely stared at her.

She smiled. "Silly question."

"I think you and your husband might derive some benefit from reading it once it's completed," said Simon. "Especially your husband."

"His name is Bob, and I don't tell him what to read," she said heatedly.

"Perhaps you ought to," said Simon.

"Come on, Simon," said Christina. "I'm only going to be here a few more days. Let's not fight."

"As you wish," said Simon, dismissing the subject and all else his sister might have to say with a single shrug, and turning to Gold. "I walked past the Vainmill Building this morning, Father."

"And?" asked Gold.

"They've changed the name of the prize from the *Velvet Comet* Challenge Cup to the Thomas Gold Challenge Cup, and turned it into a rotating trophy."

"What's a rotating trophy?" asked Gold.

"Evidently they've made a duplicate for the owner of the winning horse to keep, but the original is on display in one of their ground-floor windows, along with a life-sized holo of you, Fiona Bradley, and the madam. Evidently the cup is to be presented every year."

"Nobody ever said they were stupid," commented Gold.

"You should never have gone up there in the first place," said Simon. "I warned you against it."

"Of course I should have. We've already spent the money where it will do the most good."

"It may have done us more than ten million credits' worth of harm," said Simon.

"I doubt it," answered Gold. "Anyone who truly believes that holograph wasn't staged would believe the worst of me whether I visited the *Comet* or not." He paused. "Besides, every now and then you have to beard the lion in his own den."

"It seems that there were a lot more lionesses than lions."

"Just what is *that* supposed to mean?" demanded Gold.

"Jesus may have stopped the masses from stoning a prostitute, but he didn't feel it incumbent upon himself to visit her place of work," said Simon. "Your very presence aboard the *Velvet Comet*, no matter how much they donated to the church, lends an air of legitimacy to it."

"You make it sound like I'm one of their customers," said Gold.

"You made it *look* like you were," said his son.

"We've been through all this before," said Gold. "If I hadn't gone up there, I wouldn't have seen the aliens, and if I hadn't seen the aliens, I wouldn't have found a focus for my attacks on Vainmill."

"The end doesn't justify the means."

"I'm getting tired of arguing this with you, Simon. Pure I went and pure I returned—and what I learned while I was there will make my job much easier."

"God's work doesn't include visiting a brothel," said Simon.

"No. But mine does, and ultimately I am a servant of the Lord."

"Then you should have *acted*!" said Simon passionately. "Jesus threw the money-lenders out of the Temple. You refused even to enter the casino."

"I'm not Jesus," replied Gold. "I'm simply a man, doing the best I can. They have three hundred security guards up there. How many people do you think I could have thrown out of the casino before they stopped me?"

"You should have done *something* to show your disapproval!"

"What would *you* have done?" asked Gold.

"I wouldn't have gone there in the first place."

"Do you two go on like this every day?" asked Christina, who had been a silent but interested spectator.

"Please don't interfere, sister," said Simon.

"Every day and every night," answered Gold with a rueful smile. "We have a basic disagreement. I want to be the best man I can be. Your brother wants me to be perfect."

"The Word of God isn't subject to interpretation," said Simon. "It's right there in the Bible in black and white. It may be a harsh and demanding Word, but it's God's Word nonetheless." He looked directly into his father's eyes. "And the moment you start modifying it, or changing it out of expediency, then you have perverted what you stand for and made it meaningless."

"I can hardly argue with that," agreed Gold. "It's the basis of my faith."

"Then why did you act contrary to it?" persisted Simon.

"Because I'm not perfect," said Gold. "Because I can fight Evil much more effectively once I know the shape and face of it. And because if I didn't fight it in *my* way, sooner or later you would fight it in *yours*, and it's my duty as a father and a Christian to spare you the pain."

"There's no pain involved in serving the Lord."

"If that were so, there would be no *Velvet Comet* or Vainmill Syndicate, and no one would ever ignore the cries of the sick and the hungry," said Gold. "The path of righteousness is many things, but it is never easy."

"All the more reason not to knowingly stray from it," said Simon.

"Enough," said Gold, and something in the tone of his voice seemed to startle his son.

"As you wish," said Simon. He paused. "Will Mother need any help setting the table?"

"She's got some," said Christina.

Jeremy entered the room just then.

"Grandmother says that we're almost ready," he announced. "Hello, Uncle Simon."

"Hello, nephew," said Simon. "Did you enjoy the zoo?"

The boy nodded his head. "We're going to the aquarium tomorrow," he said happily.

"Have you ever been to one before?" asked Simon, feeling slightly awkward, as he always did when addressing children.

The boy shook his head.

"Neither have I. Let me know if you enjoy it."

"I will," promised Jeremy. "And the day after, we're going to the video studio, and I'll see Grandfather give his speech."

"His sermon," Simon corrected him.

Jeremy began rattling off his agenda for the coming week, and a moment later Corinne reentered the room.

"Jeremy, I thought I told you to bring everyone back with you." She flashed a smile to her son. "Good evening, Simon."

Simon stared at her for a moment.

"What happened to your hair?" he demanded at last.

"I styled it for her," said Christina.

"Harlots style their hair," said Simon. "Married women don't."

"*This* married woman does," Corinne replied.

"*My* hair is styled, too," added Christina. "Are you calling *me* a harlot?"

"You're wearing makeup, too, aren't you?" said Simon, ignoring his sister's comments.

"Yes, I am," his mother replied.

"Leave her alone," said Christina hotly.

"Decent women don't paint their faces," said Simon.

"When I'm in the sanctity of my own home, I'll wear what I like," said Corinne. "And before you start quoting what the Bible says about painted women, maybe you'd better reread what it says about addressing your parents with respect."

"I'm fully aware of what the Bible says on *both* subjects," replied Simon. "Evidently you are not."

"That's enough, Simon," said Gold ominously.

"But *you* above all people should have forbidden this!" complained Simon.

"It's not up to me to forbid it," said Gold. "Your mother is a free agent. Besides, this is a very little thing, and it makes her happy—or at least it did until a minute ago."

"There is no such thing as a *little* sin," said Simon. "Something is either sinful or it's not."

"But there *is* such a thing as free will," said Gold. "And if this is what your mother wishes to do, then I support her right to do it."

"And you don't disapprove?"

"I preferred it the old way," said Gold. "So what?"

"If you won't correct your own wife, what gives you the right to try to correct Vainmill?" said Simon.

"Since you insist on speaking about me as if I weren't here, I'll make it easier for you," said Corinne angrily. She took her grandson's hand. "Come along, Jeremy. You didn't come here to watch your uncle start a family fight." She turned on her heel and left the room, half-pulling Jeremy behind her.

"I think you owe her an apology," said Christina.

"I think she owes one to God," said Simon.

"You're both wrong," said Gold. he waited until he had their attention. "Your mother owes no one an apology. But you, Simon, have made a very decent woman unhappy. I think it's you who owes God the apology."

"Do you think God wants her painting her face and wearing her hair like that?" said Simon. "If you truly do, then I'll apologize to all parties involved."

Gold sighed. "We lead a harsh, spare existence,

Simon. I know that your mother likes music, and yet she willingly cut herself off from it when our doctrine was modified. She is a voracious reader, and yet our religion severely limits her choice of reading matter." He paused. "Most men of my stature have impressive houses and a multitude of luxuries that go along with them; but because we pass most of our personal income on to the needy, we live in this apartment, we use public transportation, and when something breaks we repair it rather than replace it. Your mother has precious few frivolous pleasures in her life; why not allow her this one?"

"You didn't answer my question," said Simon.

"Surely you don't equate her hairdo with Vainmill's treatment of aliens or ownership of the *Velvet Comet*?" said Gold.

"You still didn't answer me: Do you think God wants her wearing makeup and styling her hair?"

Gold stared at his son and sighed again. "No," he admitted at last. "No, I don't."

"Then I'll make no apology."

"And you wonder why Bob refuses to join us for dinner!" said Christina.

"The truth makes him uncomfortable," said Simon.

"*You* make him uncomfortable," replied Christina. "There's not an ounce of compassion in you."

"Your husband and I were both raised as Jesus Pures," said Simon. "The only difference is that I don't make any compromises with my beliefs."

"Neither does he!" she shot back heatedly.

"Oh, come on," said Simon. "He eats meat, he sings, he works on the Sabbath, he—"

"That's not fair!" snapped Christina. "You know why he does those things. He's an exobiologist: he spends a considerable amount of his time in the field with aliens. There are some races that can only communicate musically, just as there are some that would be offended if he didn't share their food with them."

"That's no excuse for behaving contrary to the dictates of his religion."

"Why, you pompous ass!" she exploded. "You sit around beating your breast about our shabby treatment of aliens, and when somebody actually goes out and tries to do something about it, you climb into you pulpit and condemn him! I don't have to listen to this kind of drivel!"

She walked out of the room.

"Do you plan to drive *me* out of the room, too?" inquired Gold dryly. "Or do you think you might calm down a little?"

"I'm perfectly calm," answered Simon.

"You seem to be in a minority," remarked Gold.

"I will ask you again: was anything I said false?"

"No."

"Well, then?"

"Simon, I agree with you that there are no degrees of sin," began Gold. "One either breaks God's laws or one doesn't. But there *are* degrees of commitment."

"Commitment?" asked Simon, puzzled.

"Commitment," repeated Gold. "None of us is perfect. We all break God's laws, even you. But there is a clearly discernible difference between a Fiona Bradley, who has made a clear commitment to perpetuating Vainmill's corporate sins, and your mother and brother-in-law, who are well-intentioned but occasionally slip from Grace."

"All of them are wrong," said Simon stubbornly.

"True. But not all of them are evil. Jesus could differentiate between a Magdalene and the Pharisees; I think it's about time you learned to do the same. When your mother wears makeup every day, or Robert eats steak and sings songs when he is not in the company of aliens, that will be ample time to condemn their souls to everlasting perdition."

"And if you don't stop Mother now, then the day will come when she paints her face every morning."

"I sincerely doubt it," said Gold. "And if she does, then she will have made her choice and will have to suffer the consequences."

"Sin isn't quantitative or qualitative," protested Simon. "It either exists or it doesn't—and if it does, then it must be condemned." He began pacing back and forth. "I'm only quoting *you*, Father. This is what you've taught me all my life. This has been at the heart of every sermon you've ever given!"

"I know," said Gold.

"Then why are we having this disagreement?"

"Because God only created one perfect man, and I have a certain amount of compassion for those imperfect creatures that I happen to love."

"You love Robert?" said Simon sardonically. "Next you'll be telling me you love Fiona Bradley."

"No, I don't love Robert," said Gold. "I hardly know him. But I love Christina, and he makes her happy. And I love Jeremy, and he helped to make Jeremy."

Simon shook his head. "By the same token, you have to love Robert's mother and father, since they created him. Or, to take a more interesting hypothesis, what if Robert has a mistress? If she makes him happy, then he in turn will be better disposed to make Jeremy happy. Should you love his mistress?"

"Of course not. Each of us has to draw the line somewhere. I've drawn mine."

"And I mine," said Simon stubbornly.

Gold shook his head. "You've drawn a tight little circle that only has room for one person in it: Simon Gold. And I have a feeling you'll be harder on him than on anyone else when he finally falls from Grace."

"He doesn't have to fall," replied Simon. "*You* didn't."

"I do every day," said Gold. "The only difference between me and Fiona Bradley is that I regret it."

"There's another: you succeed in overcoming your weaknesses."

"Not always," said Gold wryly. "In the heat of the moment I even made a bet on the horserace."

"So you told me," said Simon. "I think that supports my argument about the *Velvet Comet*. If even Thomas Gold could fall prey to its siren song, then no moral man should ever set foot aboard it."

"Perhaps you're right," said Gold after some consideration. "We'll discuss it further after dinner." He got to his feet. "In the meantime, I think it's time you made peace with your mother and sister. I'm getting hungry."

"All right," said Simon. He paused. "I really didn't mean to make her angry, you know."

"I know," said Gold. He put his arm around his son's shoulders and had begun walking to the dining room when the house computer announced that there was someone without the lock combination at the front door. He began retracing his steps, only to find that Christina had gotten there ahead of him.

"Who is it?" asked Gold after a moment, when nobody had entered the apartment.

Christina turned to him with a puzzled expression. "She wouldn't leave her name. She just placed this in my hand and told me to make sure you got it." She held up a small, flat package.

Gold walked over and took the package from her, examining it for writing or coding and finding none.

"What do you suppose it is?" she asked, curious.

"Unless I miss my guess, it's the reason twenty-seven Jesus Pures were incarcerated on Delvania," answered Gold.

Her face reflected her interest. "Really?"

"I can't imagine what else it could be," replied Gold. "You're sure she didn't say anything else?"

"Nothing."

"Did she look familiar?"

"No."

Simon returned from the dining room. "What's going on?" he asked. His gaze fell on the package. "Is that what I think it is?"

"Probably," said Gold.

"Who delivered it?" continued Simon.

"I don't know. She didn't leave her name, and Christina didn't recognize her."

"What's in it?" asked Christina. "What's all this about twenty-seven Jesus Pures being incarcerated?"

"The *Velvet Comet* has a training school on Delvania," began Gold.

"A training school?" repeated Christina disbelievingly.

Gold nodded. "And in this school, along with all the men and women, they have six Andricans." He paused. "Somebody—probably a Jesus Pure, though we don't know that for sure—found a way to tap into their computer on Delvania, and lifted copies of their work contracts, as well as some footage of the more exotic training sessions they've been forced to undergo. Vainmill responded by arresting the entire Jesus Pure colony on the planet, though they released them a few hours later."

"You had nothing to do with this?" asked Christina.

"Of course not," said Gold. "I'm offended that you should think otherwise."

"I only asked because you know what's in it, and you don't seem very surprised that it was delivered to you."

"I know what's in it because a man named Gustave Plaga contacted me and accused me of having stolen it," said Gold. "As for my lack of surprise at receiving it, I'm the logical person to give it to. I can make better use of it than anyone else can." He stared at the package and frowned. "I don't approve of the means by which it came into my possession, but it could be just the thing I need to get those aliens off the *Velvet Comet* and out of the training school."

"I think you should return it," said Simon.

Gold shook his head. "I've been looking for something like this for five years."

"It's immoral material, immorally obtained," said Simon. "If you have to stoop to Vainmill's level, then the battle is not worth winning."

"And what of the faeries?" demanded Gold. "Should I just let them continue to work as indentured prostitutes and forget about them?"

"Of course not. But if you're to wage God's battle, you must fight by God's rules."

"God tells me to fight injustice wherever I find it," responded Gold firmly. "That's just what I plan to do."

"I think you're making an enormous mistake," said Simon.

"I'd be making a less forgivable mistake if I have the means to free the Andricans from their servitude and do nothing about it."

"May I say something?" interjected Christina.

"Go ahead," said Simon. "Side with *him*."

"I think he's wrong," she replied

Father and son both looked surprised.

She turned to Gold. "This package contains stolen property. Since you had nothing to do with the theft of this material, your hands are clean. But the instant you try to use it, you might be legally culpable."

"It's a chance I'll have to take," said Gold. "However, I doubt that they'll prosecute; it would entail too much additional bad publicity. Besides, when I make it public, it will be analogous to a journalist making a story public—even to the point of maintaining the confidentiality of my source, whose name I truly don't know. What do you think, Simon?"

"You know what I think."

"I mean about the legal ramifications."

"I'm more concerned with the moral ramifications," said Simon.

"If you see a number of men abusing a helpless child, and God places a sword in your hand, is it immoral to use it?" responded Gold.

"God didn't put that package in your hand," said Simon. "A common thief did."

"Or possibly a divinely inspired one," said Gold. "God cannot want Vainmill to continue subjugating aliens. Possibly this entire chain of events *was* His doing."

"You don't know that."

"You don't know that it wasn't," replied Gold. "I have been given the sword. I *have* to use it."

"You insist?" asked Simon.

"I do."

"Then, if I can't dissuade you, at least let one of your subordinates examine the contents."

"Why?"

"Because I don't think you should be forced to subject yourself to scenes of sexual degradation."

"Nobody's forcing me," said Gold. "But if I gave it to one of my assistants, *I'd* be forcing *him*." He slipped the package into a pocket. "Try to wipe that look of consternation off your face. One would think that this"—he patted his pocket—"was Pandora's Box instead of Joshua's Trumpet."

"Let's hope it isn't," said Simon.

"It isn't," Gold assured him. "Now let's have dinner—I'm famished. Christina, go into the kitchen and ask you mother to come out and join us." He turned to Simon. "Personally, I don't care whether you apologize to your mother for your behavior or not—but she'd better *think* that you're apologizing."

Gold's children accompanied him to the dining room, where Jeremy was playing with an electronic toy. A moment later Simon was carefully explaining to his mother, in the exceptionally precise language he used for such occasions, just what it was that he hadn't meant, while Gold attacked his dinner and tried to ignore the sudden surge of excitement he felt at the thought of reviewing the material in the package.

5

"Well, son of a bitch, it's old Good as Gold!"

Gold emerged from the seemingly endless labyrinth he had been traversing and found himself in a strange, moonlit valley. Insects roared like carnivores, snakes whistled like birds, carnivores grazed on purple grass, mermaids slithered up trees, and gryphons with gills swam in a nearby brook.

He looked down a long, tortuously twisting path and saw a small green imp sitting on the low-hanging limb of a gnarled tree.

"Who are you?" he demanded. "What are you doing here?"

"Calm down, Tom baby," said the imp, taking a bite of an apple. "Otherwise you're going to have a stroke, and no doubt about it."

"I don't approve of your language," said Gold severely.

"Yeah?" retorted the imp. "Well, at least I'm wearing pants."

Gold inspected himself and found to his surprise that he was totally nude. He immediately raced behind a large flowering shrub to hide his nakedness, and bumped *into a nude girl with transparent wings. She took one look at him, giggled, and flew away.*

"By the way," said the imp, suddenly appearing beside him and swinging his enormous penis like a lariat, "I lied to you." He flashed Gold a toothy grin. "Nobody wears pants around here."

"I guess nobody does," agreed Gold, staring at a Homerically endowed blue gnome that popped into existence a few yards away.

"Well, now that you're here, we've got things to do and places to go," said the imp. "How are you at riding unicorns?"

"I don't know."

"Well, there's only one way to find out."

Instantly Gold found himself atop a sleek, sweat-covered unicorn. It was dark, almost black, and seemed to fight against his restraint.

"I've seen this one before," said Gold. "In a race, I think."

"Anything's possible," said the imp. "Especially around here."

"Anyway, I've seen him," said Gold, as the dark unicorn began racing across the constantly changing landscape. Small trees swayed as he raced by them. "He was named for a city."

"Enjoying the ride?" asked the imp, now half his former size, perching on Gold's shoulder.

"It feels . . . good," said Gold thoughtfully, concentrating on the muscular body that was moving rhythmically between his naked legs.

"Hold still," cautioned the imp.

"But I have to move as the unicorn moves," explained Gold patiently, matching the motions of his body to those of his mount. "Otherwise I'll fall off."

"You keep moving like that and you'll wake Corinne," warned the imp.

"*Corinne? Where is she?*"

"*Sleeping right next to you. Snoring her head off, as usual.*"

"*I'll be quiet,*" said Gold, still moving his body in rhythm with the racing unicorn.

"*Quiet's got nothing to do with it. You keep moving and you'll wake that frigid bitch up and then you'll never get where you're going.*"

"*Don't talk about her like that!*" snapped Gold. "*She's my wife!*"

"*Well, mercy me!*" said the imp sarcastically. "*Aren't we high and mighty tonight? The famous Thomas Gold can walk around naked and practically drill a hole in my favorite unicorn's neck, and I can't tell him the truth about his wife. A thousand pardons, sahib!*"

Gold found himself on the ground again, his body once again coming under his control.

"*All right, no unicorns,*" he said regretfully. "*What now?*"

"*What do you suppose?*"

"*I don't know,*" said Gold.

"*You're a liar,*" replied the imp.

"*I really don't know.*"

"*If you really mean that, pinch yourself and maybe you'll wake up.*"

"*No,*" said Gold quickly, turning a bright red and desperately willing himself to remain asleep.

"*Then maybe I'll pinch you myself,*" said the imp, reaching for Gold's groin.

"*No!*" shrieked Gold, leaping back and sprawling on the grass.

"*Such concern!*" said the imp mockingly. "*I can't imagine why: you never use the damned thing anyway.*"

"*I'll bet he does,*" said a sultry voice, and Gold turned to find an enormous nude woman approaching him. Her breasts practically blotted out the sky, and her legs were

*covered by hand-painted directional arrows, all pointing
to her genitals.*

"Help me!" Gold cried desperately, reaching his hand
out to the imp.

"Happy to," said the imp. "I'll take the front, you take
the back—or the other way around. Anything for a pal."

"Make her go away!"

"Nothing to it," said the imp, waving his hands in the
air. "Abracadabra."

The enormous woman keep approaching.

"Son of a bitch," said the imp with a shrug. "That
always worked before."

"Help me!" pleaded Gold again.

"I thought God helped those who helped themsleves,"
remarked the imp with a grin. "Or is that all bullshit?"

"Don't make fun of the Lord!" bellowed Gold. "That's
blasphemous!"

"My apologies," said the imp with a sardonic bow. "I
keep forgetting that you're a moral man."

Gold got to his feet and began running. As he did so,
the ground became softer and softer, until he was mired
in it up to his thighs. He looked back and could find no
sign of the gigantic woman.

"Well done, Tom," said the imp, suddenly appearing
on his shoulder again. "The Church Elders would have
been proud of you."

"Get me out," said Gold.

"I can't."

"You mean you won't," said Gold bitterly, futilely
attempting to move his legs.

"Can't," repeated the imp. "You're stuck here forever."

"But I ran away from her," protested Gold. "I turned
my back on temptation. It's not fair!"

"Well, it's easy to be moral when a giant wants to use
you as a dildo," said the imp. "How are you with people
your own size?"

"I've been a good husband," said Gold. "I've never cheated. I've never known any woman but Corinne."

"Lucky you," said the imp, unimpressed. He waved a hand and a score of nude women appeared. "What do you think, Tom baby?"

"I'm a God-fearing, moral man!" cried Gold. "I can't be having a dream like this!"

"So you keep saying," chuckled the imp.

"Take them away!" said Gold, trying to ignore the sudden stirring in his loins.

"Still too big for you?" asked the imp, as the women vanished. "How about something even smaller?" he suggested meaningfully.

"No," said Gold. "I'm a decent man. Why are you doing this to me?"

"This isn't my dream, Tom baby; it's yours. I'm not doing a thing." The imp seemed amused. "Now be honest with me: you want to see what comes next, don't you?"

"No."

"Tell the truth and I'll let you out."

"Yes," said Gold, feeling a secret excitement.

Suddenly two more green imps appeared, one of each sex.

"Beautiful, aren't they?" asked the imp.

"They look like toads," said Gold, strangely disappointed.

"Toads croak, Tom," said the imp. He nodded his head, and the two imps began whistling melodically.

"I've heard it somewhere before," said Gold. "It sounds beautiful."

"Beauty is in the eye of the beholder, Tom," said the imp. "Tell me what you see."

Gold looked at the two imps again, and suddenly found himself staring at Oberon and Titania.

"I see toads," he lied. "I am a servant of God, and I see toads."

"Come closer, children," said the imp, and the two

*faeries obeyed. "Now, take a good look at this, Tom,"
continued the imp, running his hand over Titania's
breasts. "Does this look like a toad to you? No warts at
all." He slid his hand down over her belly and inserted a
finger into her vagina. She giggled and whistled a
seductive tune. "Do you think I could do this to a
toad, Tom?"*

"No," said Gold hoarsely, unable to move a muscle.

*"You've been looking for heaven too high up and too
far away, Tom," continued the imp. He withdrew his
finger and gave Titania's vulva a friendly pat. "It's
been right here all along."*

*"We will both be stricken dead," said Gold miserably.
"You for saying it and me for listening."*

*"Does this one look like a toad, too?" continued the
imp, fondling Oberon's penis.*

*Gold shook his head. "This is immoral," he said at
last. "I shouldn't be watching this."*

"Then close your eyes."

"I can't," said Gold, making a futile attempt to do so.

"I'll bet Simon could," said the imp. "Couldn't he?"

*"Yes," said Gold, feeling totally humiliated by the
truth of his answer.*

*The imp took a step back, and Oberon and Titania
began approaching Gold.*

"Leave me alone!" he shouted.

*"You don't mean that, Thomas," said Titania and
Oberon in unison, and he suddenly noticed that they
were no longer whistling but were speaking actual words.*

*"The Lord is my shepherd, I shall not want," intoned
Gold, trying to look to the sky but unable to tear his
fascinated gaze from the faeries.*

"None of us want Him, Thomas," crooned Titania.

"Get thee behind me, Satan!" screamed Gold.

"So that's the way he likes it!" laughed the imp.

"*Leave me alone!*" stammered Gold. "*I'm not an evil man! I've got to wake up!*"

"*Why?*" asked Titania.

"*Why?*" asked Oberon.

"*Why, indeed?*" asked the imp.

"*Because you want me to fall from the path of righteousness.*"

"*Fall from it?*" chuckled the imp. "*You're mired in it up to your knees.*" He leered at Oberon and Titania. "*Admit it, now—wouldn't you like to violate them? Just a little?*"

"*Violate,*" crooned Titania.

"*No!*" cried Gold. He tried once more to close his eyes, but found that they still wouldn't obey his commands.

Two more nude faeries popped into existence.

"*If you don't like them, how about us?*" they asked.

"*No!*"

Four more faeries suddenly appeared. "*You're right. They're no good,*" they said, each mouthing a word in turn. "*Come try us.*"

"*Never!*" yelled Gold. "*I am a man of God!*"

"*You know, Tom,*" said the imp, "*I could make you a group price on all eight.*"

"*Buy all eight,*" said Oberon enticingly.

Titania licked her lips slowly. "*Violate,*" she whispered.

"*Once you've had them, the mystery will be gone,*" said the imp, with the air of one who knew. "*The urge will vanish, the flesh will be slave to the spirit once more, and you can destroy the ship—annihilate it.*"

"*Buy all eight,*" urged Oberon.

"*Violate,*" breathed Titania.

"*Annihilate,*" promised the imp.

"*Buy all eight, violate, annihilate,*" chanted the faeries. "*Buy all eight, violate, annihilate,*" they sang over and over again.

"*Stop it!*" Gold managed to scream.

"*Come on, Thomas,*" said Titania, striking an obscene pose. "*There's nothing to it but to do it.*"

"*I can't!*" cried Gold. "*I took a vow of fidelity!*"

"*But you come here every night after Corinne is asleep,*" persisted Titania.

"*Never!*" said Gold.

"*Every night since we first met,*" said Titania. "*You may not remember it, but we do.*"

"*Bring Corinne along next time,*" said Oberon with a knowing leer. "*We can all have a party.*"

"*No!*" screamed Gold. "*This has got to stop!*"

"*Then leave,*" said the imp, vastly amused.

Gold tried to move and found that he was still paralyzed.

"*I can't,*" he said miserably.

"*Then you'll just have to take the consequences,*" said the imp, licking his lips and fondling his penis again.

"*Do you like my eyes?*" asked Titania.

"*My size?*" asked Oberon proudly.

"*My thighs?*" asked Titania.

"*My lips?*" asked Oberon.

"*My hips?*" asked Titania.

"*Oh, God, leave me alone!*" whispered Gold, hoping they wouldn't hear him.

Titania approached him. "*Just relax and enjoy,*" she crooned, running her hands over his body.

"*Even if it's immoral,*" added Oberon, joining her.

"*Oh, yes, it's immoral,*" agreed Titania, brushing her lips across Gold's.

"*But enjoyable,*" said Oberon.

"*Enjoyable,*" whispered Titania.

"*But immoral,*" whispered Oberon.

"*What will people say when they find out?*" asked Gold. "*What will they think of me? What will Corrine think?*"

"*No one will ever know,*" said Titania, kneeling down in front of him.

"*I'll know. Even after I wake up, I'll know.*"

"The way you lie to yourself?" laughed the imp.

"This time I'll know," said Gold with conviction.

"Fat chance," said the imp.

"And God will know," said Gold, suddenly more terrified than he had ever been in his life.

"Then we'll invite Him to the party too," said Oberon, kneeling down behind him.

"No!" said Gold, horrified, as the faeries's hands and mouths continued to explore his body. *"This is wrong!"*

"What has right or wrong got to do with it?" asked the imp. *"All that matters is that this is what you want."*

"No! It's not what I want! It can't be what I want!"

"Then why do you keep coming back here night after night?"

"I don't!"

"You don't what?"

"I don't know!" moaned Gold.

"I do," giggled Titania. *"It's the same reason you think about us for hours every day."*

"Every day," echoed Oberon.

"Hours and hours," said Titania.

"Every day," said the faeries.

"I don't!"

"You do," persisted the imp.

"Hardly ever," said Gold, trembling.

"All the time," said the imp. *"Would you like to know the reason why?"*

"NO!" screamed Gold.

"What's the reason?" asked the faeries.

"What is it, Thomas?" asked Oberon.

"What is it, Thomas?" asked Titania.

"What is it what is it what is it?" demanded the faeries.

"What is it, Thomas?" asked Corinne, shaking him by the shoulder.

Gold sat up, his nightclothes drenched with sweat.

He looked around, panic-stricken, and as he slowly realized where he was his breathing gradually became normal.

"Are you all right?"

He nodded. "Just a bad dream," he managed to mutter, painfully aware of the fact that he had an erection. He kept his legs bent beneath the covers so that Corinne wouldn't notice it.

"You've been having them for more than a week, Thomas," she said, her voice and face reflecting deep concern. "Perhaps you should see a doctor."

"I'll be all right."

"But—"

"No!" he shouted. Then he realized he had yelled at her, and he touched her hand, feeling none of the electricity at the contact of flesh upon flesh that he had felt in his dream. "I'm sorry. I'm still waking up."

"Can I get you anything?" asked Corinne.

"No," he said, swinging his feet to the floor as he felt his erection beginning to subside. "I guess I've just been working too hard."

"A sleeping pill, perhaps?" she suggested.

He had to restrain himself from yelling at her again. "No, thank you," he said, forcing a tight smile to his lips. "I don't think I want to go back to sleep just now."

"You're sure?"

"Positive."

"Well, I guess I'll put on my robe and sit up with you," she said, getting up and starting to walk to the closet.

"Don't bother," he said. "I'll be all right, I assure you."

"It's no bother, Thomas," she replied. "I love you. I'm happy to do it."

"I know," said Gold. He stood up and ran his hands through his hair, then looked down ruefully at his nightclothes. "I'm soaked," he said. "I think I'd better take a shower."

"Will you be coming back to bed then?" asked Corinne.

"Not right away. I'll probably do a little reading."

"But it's the middle of the night."

"I'm not sleepy. I think I heard once that keeping unusual hours was one of the banes of late middle age."

"I never heard that," said Corinne.

"Well, I think it's going to be the bane of *mine* for the time being."

She looked at him. "I'm worried about you, Thomas."

He walked over and kissed her on the forehead. "Just pray for me," he said. "I'll be fine."

He folded his robe over his arm, left the bedroom, ordered the door to close behind him, and walked down a short hallway to the apartment's single bathroom. He commanded the door to shut and lock behind him, ordered the shower to activate, and took off his nightclothes.

He stepped into the shower, scrubbed his body thoroughly, avoiding contact with his genitals, and rinsed himself, muttered "Off," and reached for a towel as the flow of water subsided.

As he dried himself, he dared a look into the mirror and found, almost to his surprise, that he hadn't sprouted horns and a tail since dinner. He leaned closer to the mirror and studied the face that stared out at him. It was gaunt and strong, with frank brown eyes and a jawline that had become accentuated over the years. He looked for the sign of weakness that he feared, but couldn't detect it. It was just a face like any other, a little more distinctive perhaps, but in no way unique.

He sighed, donned his robe, ran a comb half-heartedly through his hair, and ordered the door to open. He walked to the kitchen, decided that he wasn't hungry after all, and wandered into the living room. He picked up a large, leather-bound copy of the Bible from its wooden book stand—most of his literature was in the computer's library bank, but he liked the heft and feel of the Bible—and sat down in his favorite easy chair.

He thumbed through it aimlessly, reading a paragraph here and there, unable to concentrate on anything until he came to the Song of Solomon, and when he suddenly realized that he had been reading it with rapt attention he slammed the book shut and replaced it on the stand.

He checked the kitchen again, found that he still wasn't hungry, and began wandering through the apartment, reading the various plaques and commendations he had received from the Jesus Pures and other religious organizations, staring thoughtfully at the numerous holographs of himself addressing his congregation or his vast video audience.

And finally, when he had examined every inch of the kitchen and the dining room and the living room and the hallways, and was sure that Corinne was asleep, he walked to the apartment's other bedroom, which had been converted into a study, activated the computer, and sat down to prepare his sermon. He made three or four false starts, erased them all, and finally decided, with a growing tension in his loins, that he would have to study the material from Delvania once more before he could determine the best way to incorporate it into his broadcast.

The contracts were easy, of course; he would display them for half a minute or so, explain the more onerous clauses, and then turn them over to his legal staff to see if they were actually valid or if there was a chance that the courts might overturn them.

The training sessions were another matter, however. There was some awfully strong footage in there, some things that people who were morally weaker than himself had no right to see. Probably the best thing to do was review it thoroughly and decide what could and could not be disseminated to the masses.

With an unsteady voice, he ordered the computer to bring the training sessions up for his dispassionate analysis.

He spent the next two hours staring, unblinking, at the holographic images.

"Welcome back, Tom," said the imp. *"We've been waiting for you."*

"What am I doing here?" demanded Gold, lowering his hands to hide the evidence of his arousal.

"You fell asleep at the computer," answered the imp with an amused laugh.

"Where's the unicorn?" asked Gold. *"The one that looks like the racehorse?"*

"He's not in this dream."

"But he's always here," protested Gold. *"I want to ride him."*

"I thought you couldn't remember your dreams, Tom," said the imp.

"Now I can," said Gold, flustered.

"Well, we seem to be cutting out the preliminaries this

time—but don't ask me why. After all, it's your dream, not mine."

"Where are they?" asked Gold, trying to hide his eagerness.

"Where are who?" asked the imp with a grin.

"You know."

"No I don't, Tom," answered the elf teasingly. "Tell me who you're talking about."

"I can't."

"Then I can't help you."

"You've got to!" said Gold desperately. "Corinne will wake me up any minute!"

"All right, Tom," said the imp. "Because I'm your friend, I'll help you out. Just tell me who you want to see and what you want them to do when they get here."

"I can't."

"Sure you can. It's written all over your face already."

"Please don't make me do it!" begged Gold.

"No choice, Tom. You'd better hurry up—I think Corinne's starting to stir."

And Gold, tears of humiliation running down his face, told the imp exactly what he wanted to happen next, and prayed that God's attention was momentarily directed elsewhere.

6

Richard Constantine stepped out of the elevator and into Fiona Bradley's new office, which was on the 140th floor of the Vainmill Building. A polished buttonwood desk, the largest he had ever seen, dominated the room. There were six chairs, all more comfortable than the ones on the eighty-sixth floor, and a number of ashtrays as well—another thing that had been missing from the former chairman's office. The beige carpet was plush and deep, and the one of the interior walls housed a functional fireplace, one of the few he had seen on Deluros VIII, where wood was in short supply and environmentalists were in political ascendancy. A long section of one wall had been replaced with floor-to-ceiling windows, affording a view of the city very similar to that in Fiona's apartment two floors above.

He checked his timepiece to make sure that he wasn't early, shrugged, and began looking at some of the memorabilia on the walls. There were holographs of Fiona at various stages of her career, usually in the company of some political or financial celebrity, as well as holos of her long-dead husband and two grown sons. On a shelf to the left of the fireplace was a leather-bound copy of the financial thesis that had earned her her doctorate; it was flanked by the diploma itself, and a plaque declaring her to be the honorary governor of Gamma Leporis IX, a mining world which had been abandoned until she found a way to make it profitable.

He was still examining holographs and certificates when Fiona entered the room.

"Good afternoon, Richard," she said. "I hope I haven't kept you waiting."

"Only a couple of minutes," he said.

"I had a meeting with the head of Manufacturing, and it went a little long," said Fiona. "We have some truly remarkable projects in the works," she added enthusiastically.

Constantine waited for her to sit down, and then sought out a chair for himself.

"Well, are you acquainting yourself with Entertainment and Leisure?" asked Fiona.

He nodded. "You'll get my first set of recommendations sometime tomorrow."

"What's your analysis of the division's general health?"

He shrugged. "It's not as good as I'd like, and not as bad as I feared. There are five executives I want to release, and two more I think we should promote. And Rimwork—our video network out on the Rim—is probably beyond salvage."

"You're sure?" she asked.

"Well, given our financial resources I suppose nothing is ever really beyond salvage. But I don't think saving it is worth the money and effort it would take."

"I'll look forward to seeing your report."

"The figures are being prepared right now. Oh, and thank you for the pay raise."

"Additional responsibilities require additional compensation," she replied. She smiled wryly. "By the same token, I think I agreed a little too quickly to my own salary and stock options. There's more to this job than even *I* suspected." She paused. "In fact, I'm afraid I can only give you about twenty minutes of my time. I've still got to meet with Accounting before I go to that banquet tonight."

"Then I'll get right to the point. Did you hear Tom Gold's sermon last night?"

"Curious, wasn't it?" acknowledged Fiona.

"Very," said Constantine. "That's why I requested this meeting with you." He paused, frowning. "You know, if he'd hit us with everything he had, I don't think I'd be half as disturbed as I am now."

"How disturbed *are* you now?" she inquired.

"Very," he admitted. "Could we possibly be wrong about what was lifted from the Delvania computer?"

"I've already had Security check it out," replied Fiona. "And the answer is no, we were not wrong. Gold possesses everything we thought he possessed."

Constantine uttered a frustrated sigh. "Then I wish I knew what the hell he has in mind. I spent four hours watching that footage, and it's dynamite. We put those aliens through some pretty strange training sessions." He shook his head. "So why would he show his audience a pair of contracts that are so technical that nine-tenths of them won't understand what they're seeing, and then *not* show the training tapes? It just doesn't make any sense! I mean, hell, if he'd run just a single shot of some big hulking guy trussing one of the faeries to a bed during a bondage session, we'd probably have fifty thousand people picketing the building right now."

"You've been studying his file for the past week," said Fiona. "What do *you* think his reason was?"

"I don't know," admitted Constantine. "At first I thought he backed off because the tapes were pornographic, but that's not a good enough answer. After all, it's pretty easy to edit them. You can cut out the pornography and still have some pretty shocking footage left."

"Have you any other explanation?"

He shook his head. "None. I was rather hoping that you might have some suggestions."

"I do," she said, reaching for an engraved platinum box, pulling out an imported Altairian cigarette, and lighting it up. "I think our friend Doctor Gold has made a tactical blunder."

"How?" asked Constantine.

"I think we're being blackmailed—in a very subtle way, to be sure. Since Gold considers himself a good Christian, and a good Christian would never approach us directly and offer not to show the training footage if we'll agree to make such-and-such a concession, I suspect he's trying to make us so nervous waiting for the other shoe to drop that *we* approach *him* with an offer."

Constantine considered her statement thoughtfully for a moment, then shook his head. "I don't think so."

"Oh? Why not?"

"Because everything I've been able to learn about Gold leads me to believe that he's simply not that subtle a manipulator. He never finesses when he can attack a problem head-on."

"I don't know," said Fiona dubiously. "That's the one explanation I can come up with that fits the facts."

"It might even be right," conceded Constantine. "It just *feels* wrong. He's not the type to get you into a corner and not go for the jugular."

"All right," said Fiona. "You've studied him more thoroughly than I've had a chance to do. Can you suggest some other reason for his actions?"

"I already told you: I can't—which doesn't mean there aren't any. Maybe he feels that this stuff will be more effective if he lets it dribble out over a period of months. Also, let's not forget that he's syndicated on about five hundred worlds; maybe the bulk of them wouldn't air the program if he ran that footage. Not all worlds are as liberal as Deluros, you know." He leaned back on his chair, his face a mask of frustration. "There could be half a dozen valid reasons. Hell, for all I know, he thinks the faeries look too damned happy."

Fiona stared at him, a curious smile spreading across her face.

"Do you realize what you just said?" she asked at last.

"Evidently not." replied Constantine. "At least, I don't feel as pleased with myself as you seem to be."

"You suggested that the faeries might have looked too happy."

He looked puzzled. "It was just a thing to say. I didn't mean anything by it. I don't even think I believe it."

"I know."

"You're not seriously suggesting that *that* is the reason he withheld the tape?"

"No, of course not," replied Fiona. "But the notion of happy faeries has given me an idea." She paused and smiled at him, enjoying the puzzled expression on his round face. "Richard, I think we've wasted enough time worrying about why the tape was withheld or when he's going to run it. I think it's time to take the initiative."

"I'll bite," said Constantine. "What do you think we ought to do?" Suddenly he uttered a self-deprecating laugh. "Of course! I should have thought of it myself! We'll take the two faeries from the ship, put them on video, and let them tell everyone what a wonderful time they're having and how well we're treating them." He looked inordinately proud of himself. "That *is* your idea, isn't it?"

"Something like that," said Fiona with a look of satisfaction on her face. "It will take some preparation, though. For one thing, we'll need to decide upon a format. Because of our respect for the privacy of our patrons, we've never invited any journalists aboard the *Velvet Comet*, and I don't think this is a good time to start."

"I agree," said Constantine. "Besides, I want to make sure I control exactly what gets released, and I couldn't do that if I involved the press in this. Hell, they'd probably come up with a feature on how Vainmill tries to manage the news. Another point: whatever our finished product is, I don't think we should send it to the news media the way we passed on your little message to Gold; it would look too much like another apology." He paused. "I suppose creating some kind of documentary would be best."

"About the *Comet* or the faeries?" asked Fiona.

"Neither," he answered promptly. "If we concentrate on the brothel, the faeries won't get enough attention—and if we concentrate on *them*, it will seem too defensive, too much like a direct answer to Gold's sermon." He paused. "Just because Gold is incapable of subtlety and misdirection is no reason why *we* should be. We're still not going to mention him, or seem to be replying to him. Perhaps we'll run a feature on how the *Comet's* chefs and medics and costume designers had to adapt to the faeries, which would be one way of continually putting them on display while seeming to be concentrating on someone else. Or possibly we'll focus on how their co-workers have adjusted to them. I don't know—I'll have to give it some thought."

"We do have to move quickly," Fiona pointed out. "We can't count on Gold's holding that footage back forever."

"I know. I'll send a production crew up to the *Comet* tomorrow to get the feel of the place, and I'll get up there myself as soon as I get their reports and evaluate them—maybe four or five days from now."

"Is that really necessary?" asked Fiona. "Going yourself, I mean?"

"I think so."

"You could communicate with them by computer," she said. "The shuttle flight takes about three hours each way, and you've got an awful lot of work on your desk."

He shook his head. "I've only seen the faeries on tape—and those weren't even the ones we're going to be putting on public display. Before I put too many of my eggs into one basket, I want to meet them in the flesh." He paused thoughtfully.

"Besides, this documentary is ostensibly about the *Comet*, not the faeries, so I'd like to get up there and take a look around. Maybe something will catch my eye and give me an idea on how to mount this little classic. I'm sure our production people know their business—but it's *my* neck that's on the block, not theirs." He looked at her. "You've actually met the faeries. What are they like?"

Fiona smiled. "I was a little too busy becoming chairman to pay much attention to them." She shrugged. "They seemed like pleasant little creatures. Actually, Doctor Gold was much more interested in them than I was, though in retrospect I suppose that's completely understandable."

"Did he speak with them?" asked Constantine.

"Really, I hardly noticed them at all—and I didn't spend all that much more time on *him*. You'd have to ask the Steel Butterfly about that."

"I intend to. I gather she was his watchdog for most of the time he was up there. Maybe she can tell me something about him that everyone else has overlooked."

"Do you seriously expect the madam of the biggest brothel in the Republic to give you an insight into Thomas Gold?" she said sardonically.

He shrugged. "You never know."

She uttered an amused chuckle. "Sometimes I wonder about you, Richard."

"I wasn't being facetious. Among other things, a madam has to be a bit of a psychologist; her job is figuring out what makes people tick and anticipating their needs. And everyone has needs—even Tom Gold."

"He's managed to keep them pretty well hidden thus far," observed Fiona dryly.

"That doesn't mean they aren't there. Maybe

he'd like to spend the night with the Steel Butterfly. Maybe he's a repressed homosexual. Maybe
he's dying to order a steak in one of the restaurants. Maybe he's a compulsive gambler, or a secret drinker." He chuckled. "Hell, maybe he wants
to sneak off with one of the faeries."

"And maybe you'd better get your mind back on
your documentary, she said.

Constantine considered the various weaknesses
he had listed, rejected them all, and sighed.

"Maybe I'd better," he agreed.

7

Simon Gold walked to the door of his father's study and commanded it to open.

It remain closed.

Puzzled, he repeated the order. Nothing happened.

Finally, frowning, he reached out and knocked on the door.

"Go away!" snapped Thomas Gold's voice.

"Open the door, Father," said Simon. "I have to speak with you."

"Not now. I'm busy."

"This is urgent."

He heard his father muttering furiously to himself and ordering his computer to deactivate. Then there was a moment of silence, and finally the door dilated.

"What is it?" demanded Gold, his voice strained.

Simon stared at his father's haggard face, momentarily startled.

"Are you all right?" he asked at last.

"Of course I'm all right!" snapped Gold. "Was *that* your urgent business?"

"No," responded Simon, puzzled by his father's attitude. "It was merely a question, precipitated by the fact that you look very pale and drawn."

Gold's face softened somewhat. "I apologize for yelling at you. It's just that I'm getting sick and tired of your mother's pounding on the door every half hour and asking me when I'm going to be done."

"Why not just work with the door open?" suggested Simon, walking over to a couch that was in serious need of recovering. "You always used to."

"Do I have to work with the door open for the rest of my life, just because you have fond memories of it?" demanded Gold, the color rushing to his face. He swiveled on his chair to face his son. "My work habits are my own business, and nobody else's."

"I had no intention of offending you, Father," said Simon stiffly. "Let's let the whole subject drop."

"Fine," said Gold impatiently. "All right. You're here and I'm listening. What's so important that you had to interrupt me?"

"I just received a communication from Richard Constantine," began Simon.

"Vainmill's new head of Entertainment and Leisure?" asked Gold, frowning. "Why did he contact *you*?"

"Because your computer hasn't been accepting messages for the past three hours."

"I didn't want to be disturbed," said Gold. "What does Constantine want?"

"Have you ever heard of a man named Vladimir Kozinsky?"

"Not to my knowledge," answered Gold. "Should I have?"

"Probably not. He's an engineer from Declan IV."

"That's a long way from here."

"Well, he's here now—and he's dying."

"I'm sorry to hear that."

"And," continued Simon, "he wants you to administer the Final Blessing to him."

Gold shook his head firmly. "That's out of the question. I'm much too busy."

Simon nodded approvingly. "That's what I told Constantine you'd say. Who would you like me to send in your place?"

"Just a minute," said Gold suddenly. "What does Constantine have to do with this?"

Simon grinned. "There's a chance that some Vainmill employees may be facing a charge of murder."

"Maybe you'd better tell me exactly what happened," said Gold.

"Well, as I said, Kozinsky is from Declan IV. Evidently he's been listening to you lambasting Vainmill and the *Comet* for the past four weeks, and he finally became so incensed that he came all the way to the Deluros System, took a shuttle to the *Comet*, and tried to explode a bomb in the airlock." Simon seemed amused.

"Good God!" muttered Gold, genuinely distressed. "He didn't succeed, did he?"

Simon shook his head. "Unfortunately, no. They spotted the bomb the instant he entered the airlock."

"Of course," said Gold distractedly. "If they can scan newcomers for signs of disease, there was no way he could smuggle an explosive through." He stared sharply at his son. "What happened then?"

"I gather he went berserk and started attacking the Security team with his bare hands." Simon shrugged. "In the ensuing melee, he was mortally wounded. They've got him in their hospital, up there on the *Comet*. According to Constantine, he's too weak to move. I gather he's not expected to last out the day."

"He's on the *Comet*?" repeated Gold, a tremor of excitement in his deep voice.

"Yes. Would you like me to send Malcolm Dill up there?"

"No," said Gold.

"Who *do* you want to send?" persisted Simon.

"I'll go myself."

"But I thought you said—"

"I've changed my mind," said Gold.

"Father, there's no need for you ever to set foot on the *Comet* again," protested Simon. "We have hundreds of men and women on Deluros who can administer the Final Blessing. Why not simply send one of them?"

"Are you trying to tell me my duty?" demanded Gold hotly.

"I am simply pointing out, as I did before the horserace, that any time a man of your stature visits the *Comet* for any reason at all, you tend to legitimize it."

"Before I go I'll make sure that Constantine understands that this is a private act of mercy," replied Gold. "There will be no cameras and no publicity."

"You can't accept the word of a man like that," said Simon. "His loyalty is to Vainmill."

"It's in *his* best interest to keep this thing quiet,"

answered Gold. "If the press get their hands on this story, it's only a matter of time before some other madman tries to emulate Kozinsky. Constantine's no fool; he can see that as clearly as I can."

"Then send someone else," said Simon. "Constantine's reasons for keeping it quiet will remain just as valid, and you won't have to subject yourself to that environment again. It's an evil, sinful place."

"Then how can I send someone else up there?" asked Gold.

"Men of God have no business aboard the *Comet*." replied Simon adamantly.

"By the same token, Daniel shouldn't have entered the lion's den."

"He only did it once," said Simon doggedly. "If he'd entered it a second time, they might have torn him to shreds." He paused. "By your own admission, the one time you were there you made a wager on a horserace. Who knows what might happen if you go again?"

"If he'd listened to you, Jesus wouldn't have walked among the lepers or laid his hands on the sick," answered Gold irritably.

"He was Jesus," said Simon. "You're just a man."

"What do you think I'm going to do?" snapped Gold. "Ravish the madam?"

"The *Velvet Comet* is a house of sin and degradation, and it corrupts everything it touches. Why subject yourself to it if it's not necessary?"

"It *is* necessary—and I'm getting a little sick of having you impugn my integrity!" He glared at his son. "I'm Thomas Gold! Nothing is going to tempt me from the path of righteousness!"

"I'm not questioning your motives, Father."

"Good."

'But I *am* questioning your judgment," continued Simon. "I can see no valid reason for your going up to the *Comet*, and I can see numerous reasons for staying here."

"No valid reason?" repeated Gold. "What about giving spiritual comfort to a member of my church?"

"Kozinsky's going straight to hell no matter who gives him the Final Blessing," said Simon coldly. "You know it and I know it. He tried to kill the entire crew of the ship."

"I thought you approved," said Gold sardonically.

"Certainly not, although I understand why he tried to do it. If he had succeeded, it would have meant that God approved of his methods. The fact that he failed simply means that God prefers your method of fighting the *Comet*—and *that* in turn means that Kozinsky was trying to commit murder and will burn for all eternity."

"That's one of the more farfetched rationalizations I've ever heard," said Gold.

"Just because he's a member of the Church of the Purity of Jesus Christ doesn't make his behavior acceptable," answered Simon.

"And just because his behavior is unacceptable doesn't mean that we have to turn our backs on him. He's a dying man, and he needs spiritual comfort."

"Father, may I speak frankly?" said Simon.

"That's what I thought you were doing," replied Gold with more than a trace of irony.

"You've not been yourself since you returned from the *Comet*," said Simon, ignoring Gold's comment. "You lapse into silences at odd times, you've lost weight, Mother tells me you have trouble sleeping more than a few hours at a stretch, you have nightmares, you—"

"Your mother talks too much," said Gold.

"She's worried about you," said Simon. "So am I."

"You wouldn't even know about my weight loss or my nightmares if she hadn't told you."

"But I'd know you had accepted stolen goods into your house, and had not condemned the people who committed the robbery," continued Simon.

"I thought we'd been over that before," said Gold.

"We have," said Simon. He stared directly into his father's eyes. "I'm simply trying to point out that before you went to the *Velvet Comet* you had no trouble sleeping, and that you would never consider condoning the theft of anyone's property, even your enemy's. Even your work habits have changed—you lock yourself in your room, you spend hours with your computer without producing anything, you don't answer your messages. Furthermore, you've become positively single-minded about the Andricans. You've spoken about them to the exclusion of all else during your last three sermons." He paused for breath, then continued: "I don't know what you saw aboard the *Comet*, but obviously it has had a detrimental effect on you."

"I appreciate your concern," said Gold, "but you're reading too much into the natural infirmities of late middle age. Most men my age have some trouble with their sleep and their digestion. It's nothing out of the ordinary. In fact, for a man of my years, I would say that I'm in remarkably good health. As for the faeries, they're a very weak link in Vainmill's defenses; I'd be crazy *not* to keep talking about them." He stared at his son. "Despite what you may think, my five hours aboard the *Velvet Comet* really haven't turned me into a mental and physical wreck."

"Perhaps," said Simon. "But I still think you should stay here." He paused uneasily.

"Yes?" said Gold.

"It means so much to me that I will volunteer to go in your place."

"*No!*" exploded Gold.

"But—"

"Nobody's keeping me away from them!" snapped Gold furiously. "Not you, not your mother, not anyone!"

"*Them?*" repeated Simon, puzzled. "What are you talking about?"

Gold blinked his eyes very rapidly for a moment, as if he were as confused as his son.

"Them?" he repeated. "I meant *him*, of course. Nobody is keeping me away from Kozinsky," he concluded lamely.

Simon stared at him. "It's the faeries, isn't it?" he said suddenly.

"I don't know what you mean," said Gold uneasily. "We're talking about Vladimir Kozinsky."

"No," said Simon decisively. "We're talking about the faeries."

"*You* may be," said Gold, trying to hide the sudden panic that gripped him. "*I'm* not." *Not my son, Lord*, he prayed silently; *Dear God, please don't let my son find out!*

"You're planning to smuggle them off the *Comet*!" exclaimed Simon. "You're just using Kozinsky as a subterfuge!"

"I'm going up there to give the Final Blessing to a dying man," said Gold.

"I'm not the enemy," said Simon in pained tones. "You can confide in me."

"All right," said Gold, grasping at the straw Simon had unwittingly offered him. "The thought of taking the faeries off the ship has crossed my mind."

"I should have guessed!" said Simon. "What other reason could you possibly have for wanting to go up there?"

"None," agreed Gold. He noticed that his hands were starting to shake, and he thrust them into his pockets. *Let him believe it, Lord!*

"You'll never get away with it," said Simon.

"I think I will," said Gold. He tried to force a confident smile to his lips, found that he couldn't manage it, and settled for staring defiantly at his son.

Simon shook his head. "You've already described their security system to me. You certainly can't sneak them off without anyone knowing."

"There are other ways," said Gold, his mind racing to create a believable plan of action.

"You don't even know for a fact that they'll be willing to come with you," continued Simon. "After all, you'll look like just another customer to them."

Gold stared at his son, unable to come up with even a mildly acceptable answer.

"And even if they did," persisted Simon, "you've still got to get them through the airlock, and onto a ship or a shuttle." He sighed heavily. "I don't think you've got the ghost of a chance. I've got a feeling that their Security team will be watching every move you make."

Simon continued analyzing the situation, coming up with more and more reasons why his father's nonexistent plan was doomed to failure, and Gold began to relax as Simon moved further and further from his real reason for going up the *Comet.*

Thank you, God. I'm a moral man, and I have the strength to subdue this evil within me—but not if I had to face the comdemnation in his eyes.

"The odds are a thousand to one against it," concluded Simon some five minutes later. "And even if you could succeed in removing them from the ship, they might be of more use to us right where they are, where we can keep their plight in the public eye."

"You're right," said Gold, with an sense of infinite relief. "It was a bad idea."

"Then whom shall we send to the *Comet*?"

"I'll go. I may have been wrong about helping the Andricans to escape, but there's one thing I was right about: I can't in good conscience send anyone else up there."

"You're sure?" asked Simon.

"I am." He looked directly at his son. "Unless you'd like to continue arguing the point?"

"No," said Simon with a sigh of resignation.

"Good."

Gold stared at his son for a moment, then ordered his computer to contact Richard Constantine. An hour later he was en route to the *Velvet Comet*, his mind dwelling upon his own personal demons rather than those that might be lusting for Vladimir Kozinsky's confused and darkened soul.

8

"Where are we?" asked Gold, surveying the wide, dimly lit corridor that seemed to stretch to infinity in both directions.

"In the service area beneath the Mall," replied the Steel Butterfly. "This is where the *Comet*'s supplies are delivered. In fact, they kept the race-horses down here."

"It must have been a different area," said Gold. "This doesn't look at all familiar." He paused. "What's that noise I hear overhead?"

"The tramway."

"I don't remember any tramway," said Gold. "Did you remove it for the race?"

"It's on a different level." She smiled. "Besides, you were on public display. We had orders to walk you everywhere."

"Then why aren't we riding it now?"

"Because this time I have instructions not to let *anyone* see you. Patrons occasionally take the tramway from the Resort to the airlock; they never come down here."

"By the way," said Gold stiffly as they walked past rows of neatly stacked, unopened cargo crates, "I hope you will believe me when I tell you that I have never met Vladimir Kozinsky, was completely unaware of his intentions, and would have done everything in my power to prevent him had I known of them."

"Of course I believe you," said the Steel Butterfly. "We may be on opposite sides of the fence, but I've never thought of you as a man who would condone murder."

He frowned. "I wish Vladimir Kozinsky had held that same opinion," he said grimly.

"I don't think he really intended to kill anyone," she replied.

"I was told that he tried to smuggle a bomb onto the ship." He looked sharply at her. "Did he or didn't he?"

"Oh, there's no question that he tried to bring the bomb aboard the *Comet*," said the Steel Butterfly. "I can show it to you later, if you like. But I don't think he planned to detonate it."

"Why would someone bring a bomb up here and *not* detonate it?" asked Gold.

"Attila—our Chief of Security—believes that he merely planned to *threaten* to blow it up unless we gave him what he wanted."

"What did he want?"

"Didn't Richard Constantine tell you?" she asked, surprised.

"No one has told me very much of anything. All I know is that he tried to smuggle a bomb aboard the ship, and that he was mortally wounded in the ensuing struggle. And that he has been asking for me, of course," he added as an afterthought.

"He wanted us to release the faeries from their

contract and send them home." She turned to him. "I know that you didn't mean to encourage this sort of action, but I must point out that he wouldn't even have known the faeries existed if it hadn't been for your sermons."

"Vainmill doesn't have a monopoly on stupidity or madness," replied Gold. "There are a lot of Vladimir Kozinskys in the universe." He paused. "But that doesn't mean I must stop confronting evil when I see it."

"Perhaps not— but if you hadn't confronted it so vigorously in this instance, Vladimir Kozinsky would be contentedly designing tools on Declan IV right at this minute. And as for Titania and Oberon," she continued, "they can't understand why anyone would think they aren't having the time of their lives up here."

"They know they were the reason he came up here?"

"Of course," replied the Steel Butterfly, walking forward once again. "If someone had tried to kidnap *me*, *I'd* want to know about it."

"What Kozinsky was trying to do was wrong, but I'd hardly call it kidnapping," said Gold.

"If you can think of a better word, I'll be happy to use it."

"How about *liberating*?"

"Why don't you ask the faeries if forcing them to leave here against their will qualifies as liberation?" she suggested.

"Perhaps I will," he replied, trying to keep the tremor out of his voice. "Where are they?"

"They'll be stopping by the hospital a little later," said the Steel Butterfly. "They want to see you."

"They do?" he said, startled. "Why?"

"Before your broadcast they were just curiosities, albeit very popular ones. Now they're celebrities. I have the distinct impression that they'd like to thank you."

"To *thank* me?"

She nodded. "They're very human in many respects—and everybody likes being famous. Even you, Doctor Gold."

He stared at her but made no comment.

They reached the hospital's storage areas, and took the freight elevator to the main level. As they emerged, Gold found himself in a luxurious reception foyer, filled with chairs and couches that would have seemed more appropriate in the brothel. The floors and walls were spotless, the metal chairs were polished and shining, and the reception desk brilliantly reflected the overhead lighting. A holographic map that was suspended in the air just to the left of the desk gave directions to the handful of private rooms, the low-gravity ward for heart patients, and the physical therapy rooms. There were certain areas on the map that were merely marked as being off limits to visitors, and he assumed that these were the operating theater and drug storage rooms.

"Impressive," admitted Gold as they passed through the foyer and entered a well-lit corridor.

"Thank you," said the Steel Butterfly. "We're quite proud of it." She signaled a door to open. "Here we are."

Gold followed her into the room.

Vladimir Kozinsky, a small, portly man in his mid-forties, lay on his back on an air-bed, his eyes closed, his breathing harsh and sporadic. He was entwined in a maze of tubes, all of which led into a network of life-support equipment. There were tubes running into his arms, into his left thigh, into his neck, into his nostrils. His hands and feet were secured to restrain him from moving and dislodging any of the apparatus that was extending his life from one moment to the next. His torso was swathed in pressure bandages, but Gold noticed that they were starting to stain with Kozinsky's blood.

There were three large machines on the far side of the bed, each with a multitude of screens displaying complex readouts that changed constantly and were totally incomprehensible to Gold.

"They subdued him, and when he managed to get his hands on one of their weapons in the struggle, they shot him," replied the Steel Butterfly. She stared at him. "What would *you* have done?"

"The same, I suppose—but I wouldn't have shot him six more times for good measure." He stared in fascination at the tubes and the stains. "I'm surprised that he's still alive."

"I'd feel a lot more compassion for him if he hadn't come up with a bomb," remarked the Steel Butterfly.

Gold bent over the dying man. "Vladimir Kozinsky!" he said in loud, clear tones. "Can you hear me?"

Kozinsky opened his eyes.

"Thomas Gold?" he whispered weakly.

"I'm right here," said Gold, laying a reassuring hand on the dying man's shoulder, then removing it quickly when he groaned at the touch.

"Would you like me to leave?" asked the Steel Butterfly.

"If you don't mind," replied Gold.

She walked to the door. "I'll be waiting for you in the lobby."

"How do I find it?"

"Just turn right when you leave the room, and follow the corridor."

Gold nodded, then turned his attention back to Kozinsky as the Steel Butterfly stepped out into the hall and ordered the door to close behind her.

"Is it really you?" asked Kozinsky. His eyelids flickered, but didn't open.

"It really is," said Gold, staring down at him. "How are you feeling?"

"I feel weak, but nothing hurts."

"You're probably all drugged up." He looked down at Kozinsky. "I'll be honest with you: they don't expect you to last out the day."

"I know," rasped Kozinsky. "That's why I asked for you. I want you to give me the Final Blessing."

"That's what I'm here for," said Gold. "But there's something I have to ask you first."

"What is it?" asked Kozinsky.

"Was it *my* sermon that led you to try to smuggle a bomb onto the *Comet*?"

Kozinsky nodded his head, then moaned in pain.

"But why?" persisted Gold. "I never advocated violence."

"Somebody's got to draw the line somewhere. I've seen what Vainmill has done to aliens out in the Declan system. When I heard about the Andricans, I decided I had to do something about it." He looked dismayed. "I thought that you, of all people, would understand and approve."

"You might have killed hundreds of men and women with that bomb," said Gold. "How could I approve of that? What purpose would it have served?"

Kozinsky coughed, then clutched his side and lay back, gasping for breath. Finally he spoke.

"It would have taught those bastards at Vainmill

a lesson. Maybe someone else would have been encouraged to go out and do the same to the new chairman."

Gold shook his head sadly. "Where does the Bible say that you have the right to take human life and administer punishment on God's behalf? Vengeance is the Lord's, not ours."

"But they're evil!" insisted Kozinsky. The effort left him gasping for breath again, and it was another half minute before he could continue. "You've been condemning them week in and week out! That's why I came to Deluros."

"I told my audience not to patronize any merchant who had a store in the Mall, or to buy any Vainmill product or use any Vainmill service," answered Gold. "I *never* exhorted people to go out and kill Vainmill employees."

"It was implicit," said Kozinsky doggedly. "You've always told us to confront evil wherever we find it."

"There's a difference between confronting evil and trying to take a human life," said Gold. "You must understand that by doing so, you have placed your soul at risk."

"But I did it for you!" Kozinsky exclaimed in a barely audible whisper.

"We live with the consequences of our actions," said Gold. "And you must die with the consequences of yours. The Lord has no use for the unrepentant."

"I hope God judges you as harshly as you judge me!" muttered Kozinsky.

"He will," replied Gold with a grim certainty.

"The Blessing!" whispered Kozinsky. "Please— while I can still hear it!"

Gold nodded. "Have courage," he said more gently. "God is not without compassion."

Kozinsky forced a smile to his lips, then lost consciousness.

"May God, in His infinite wisdom, have mercy on your soul," said Gold without much optimism, "and forgive you your transgressions."

Then he lit a small candle he had brought with him, placed it on a nightstand, and recited the Final Blessing. Kozinsky was still alive—though just barely—when he had finished.

He stood in silence for a few moments, still unable to comprehend why a Jesus Pure would come to the *Comet* with every intention of committing murder if he didn't get what he demanded. Then he remembered the faeries, and suddenly he had considerably less difficulty understanding how decent men could fall from a state of Grace.

He checked the screens on the monitoring apparatus, saw just enough fluctuation of lines and graphs to convince him that Kozinsky was still alive, and, pausing only to extinguish the candle, he walked to the door, exited the room, and walked to the entry foyer.

The Steel Butterfly was waiting for him there— and standing next to her were Titania and Oberon, their eyes wide and staring. Titania, a number of flowers carefully positioned in her silver hair, was clad in a brief and revealing outfit made of a glittering metallic fabric which gave her the appearance of some ethereal temptress straight out of Earth's mythology, while Oberon wore a toga of spun gold and resembled some half-human boy-god on Mount Olympus.

"What are *they* doing here?" asked Gold, surprised.

"I told you before: they want to meet the man who made them famous."

Titania opened her mouth to speak, and suddenly the room was flooded by a series of melodic trilling whistles.

"You forgot them again," said the Steel Butterfly with mock severity.

Titania giggled and trilled something else in her native tongue.

"I'm not going to spend the next half hour trying to figure out what you're saying," replied the Steel Butterfly. "Oberon, run over to the Home and bring back your translating devices." Oberon grinned, whistled something to Titania, and raced out the front door of the hospital. "Some of our customers find their language so fascinating that they actually request that they leave the translators behind," continued the madam, shaking her head wearily. "I don't know how I'm ever going to get them to wear them regularly."

Gold was suddenly aware that his mouth had gone completely dry, and that he was sweating profusely.

"Is there any water around here?" he rasped.

"Titania, go fetch Doctor Gold a glass of water," said the Steel Butterfly.

"I'd rather get it myself," said Gold quickly.

"As you wish," she replied with a shrug. "You'll find a lavatory right across the hall from Kozinsky's room."

Gold followed her directions, and a moment later was standing before a sink.

"Cold," he murmured, holding a handerchief beneath the flow of water that followed. He wrung it out and began wiping his face.

When he was finished, he stared at his face in

the mirror. It evinced no excitement, no unnatural longings, no immoral intent whatsoever. He spent a moment experimenting with each feature—mouth, jaw, eyes—and carefully set them into a mask of total disinterest. Finally, satisfied, he returned to the foyer.

"Oberon will be another few minutes," said the Steel Butterfly. "His quarters are almost half a mile away, and even if he took the tramway instead of the slidewalk he's still got to get up to the fifth level, find the translators, and then come back." She paused. "How is Kozinsky?"

"Unconscious," said Gold, suddenly cognizant of the fact that he was staring at Titania, but unable to tear his gaze away from her. "I have a feeling that he's not going to wake up again."

Titania, aware that she was the focus of Gold's attention, looked directly at him, trilled something, and grinned.

"What was that all about?" he asked uneasily.

"Who knows?" replied the Steel Butterfly with a shrug. She turned to Titania. "It's your own fault. If you'd stop forgetting your translator, people could carry on a conversation with you."

Titania laughed.

"Of course," said the Steel Butterfly wryly, facing Gold once again, "sometimes not being understood can be a distinct advantage. For all I know she's busily insulting both of us."

"What's her real name?" asked Gold.

"I couldn't pronounce it even if I knew it."

Titania touched her finger to her chest and uttered a brief, melodious whistle.

"She looks so human!" said Gold. "I don't know how she can make such sounds."

"She's just chattering now," said the Steel Butterfly. "You should hear her when she sings."

"How can you tell the difference?"

"Show him, Titania."

The little faerie shook her head.

"This is a hell of a time to be shy," complained the Steel Butterfly. "Usually we can't shut you up."

Titania turned to Gold, a questioning expression on her face.

"Please," said Gold, trying to hide his eagerness.

She smiled at him, looked directly into his eyes, and began to sing. The melody was slow and atonal, and her alien words sounded like the cold clear chimes of ice against fine crystal. As the tempo became faster, she began swaying her hips and torso in time with the music, while Gold, fascinated, stared at her intently with unblinking eyes. He felt that his hands were about to start shaking, and he quickly clasped them behind his back, which seemed to amuse Titania no end. She placed her own hands behind her back, which caused her pubescent breasts to jut out at him, swaying suggestively as her undulations continued.

Gold watched her for another few seconds, aware of an insistent pounding inside his head.

"*Enough!*" he yelled suddenly, startled by the volume of his own voice.

Titania stopped singing, puzzled.

"I will not be subjected to this!"

"To her singing?" asked the Steel Butterfly uncomprehendingly.

"To the lascivious display that accompanied it!" snapped Gold.

"Lascivious display?" repeated the Steel Butterfly.

"You know very well what I mean!" continued

Gold. He glared at Titania. "Did you really think your sexual posturing would affect me as it does your unsavory customers? I am a moral man, and I will not be treated in this manner!"

"Calm down, Doctor Gold," said the Steel Butterfly in a soothing voice. "I'm sure it wasn't her intent to sexually entice you. She was simply caught up in the rhythm of the music."

"Rhythm be damned!" he snapped. "She was flaunting her body at me, deliberately trying to tempt the one man in the Republic who is fighting to save her from a life of humiliation and an eternity of hellfire! I won't have it!" He thrust his jaw out and glared at Titania. "I'm immune to you, you little jade! Do your worst—it will make no difference!"

Titania, terrified, scampered to a position of safety behind the Steel Butterfly.

"You're losing control of yourself, Doctor Gold—and *I* won't have *that*," said the madam firmly.

"I will not be led from the path of righteousness!" declared Gold.

"Nobody's trying to lead you anywhere. You're overreacting, Doctor Gold. She was singing to you, not seducing you. And if anyone's overstepped the bounds of morality, it's you."

"Me?" he demanded.

"Or am I wrong about the Jesus Pures not listening to music?"

"God forgive me!" he muttered, stunned. "I forgot!"

"If Thomas Gold can forget what he believes in, can't an Andrican female sway her hips when she sings?" said the Steel Butterfly.

"I forgot!" he repeated unbelievingly. He continued to stare at Titania, his chest heaving as he gulped huge mouthfuls of air after his outburst.

Finally he turned to the Steel Butterfly.

"I want to go home now," he said weakly.

"Oberon is due back any minute."

"I don't care. Please take me to the airlock."

The Steel Butterfly shrugged. "If you wish," she said.

Suddenly her bracelet beeped.

"Just a moment," she said to Gold. "What is it, Cupid?"

"We have a problem in the casino which, in my judgment, requires your personal attention."

"Why not tell Tote Board about it?" she replied.

"Tote Board is asleep in his quarters, and I am compelled under these circumstances to contact the highest-ranking member of the *Comet*'s staff."

"I'll be there as soon as I attend to Doctor Gold."

"The problem is not serious, but it *is* urgent," said the computer.

She sighed. "All right. I'll be there immediately." She turned to Gold. "It's probably nothing more than a counter at the blackjack table, but I'm afraid I'll have to leave you."

"I don't know if I can find my way back to the cargo airlock," said Gold.

"That's all right. Titania can take you."

The little faerie trilled something and continued to hide behind the madam.

"It's all right, Titania," said the Steel Butterfly. "He won't yell at you again."

Titania peeked around the Steel Butterfly and made a delicate chirping sound.

"I won't harm you, child," said Gold.

She made a large semicircle around him and walked to the elevator, gesturing for him to follow her. She continued to watch him warily as they descended to the storage level, then turned to her left and began walking. He fell into step behind her, hypnotized by the motion of her buttocks and wishing the distance to the airlock were even longer. Finally he forced himself to stare at the floor, and tried to bring forth a mental picture of Corinne— but his mind's paintbrush, after an initial approximation of her face, kept giving her pointed ears and silver skin and small, youthful breasts.

A few minutes later Titania stopped at the airlock, but Gold, his gaze still glued to the floor, continued walking. She ran after him, trilling rapidly, and grabbed his hand.

He felt as if an electric current had shot all the way up his arm, and he jumped back, wild-eyed and trembling. This in turn startled the faerie, who also leaped back. They stared at each other for a long moment, and then she trilled again, visibly frightened, and pointed to the airlock.

He stared at it uncomprehendingly, and then the haze slowly lifted from his mind.

"Thank you," he whispered.

She forced a nervous smile and stepped back as he opened the door and walked into the airlock.

A few minutes later the private shuttle took off for Deluros VIII, with Gold as its sole passenger. He sat in the luxury section, his feet propped up on a cushioned footrest, his back muscles massaged by the almost imperceptible vibration of the seat. He stared dully at a viewscreen, his hand still tingling from the faerie's touch, desperately trying to recapture the instant in the theater of his mind. Twice he caught himself inadvertently humming her melodic song.

He should, he knew, be preparing himself to

face the righteous wrath of an outraged God, but instead he spent the entire trip wondering with an exquisitely aching eagerness if he would ever see Titania again, or perhaps even touch her once more.

9

"Doctor Gold?"

Gold stared at the holographic image that his computer had projected in front of him.

"Who are you?" he demanded.

"Richard Constantine. I've been trying to contact you for hours."

"I'm a busy man."

"So am I," said Constantine. "And I don't especially like to be kept waiting."

"Your likes and dislikes are of very little concern to me, Mr. Constantine," replied Gold.

"And what of Vladimir Kozinsky's fate? Is that of any concern to you?"

"I left the *Comet* almost eight hours ago," said Gold. "I'd be very much surprised if he's still alive."

"He died five hours ago," said Constantine.

"I want it known that he did not represent the Church of the Purity of Jesus Christ, and that we totally disown his actions."

"You don't sound terribly broken up about it," noted Constantine sardonically.

"He tried to destroy a human life—in fact, quite a number of them. This was in direct opposition to everything we believe in, and while we pray for his soul we condemn his actions." He reached for his computer controls. "And now, if you've nothing further to say . . ."

"I'm not through yet," said Constantine.

Gold leaned back and stared at his image curiously. "Go on," he said.

"What would you like done with the body?"

"You speak about it as if I had some proprietary interest in it," said Gold. "May I suggest that you contact his family on Declan IV?"

"I've tried. He seems to have no living relatives."

"Then I recommend that you dispose of it in the most efficient way possible."

"Doctor Gold," said Constantine coldly, "personally, I don't give a damn what happens to his body. But I thought I owed you the courtesy of seeing if there is any method that is preferred by your church—or if there is any particular means of disposal that would cause distress to a Jesus Pure."

"I apologize," said Gold. "We have no particular strictures—burial and cremation are both acceptable."

"Then, with your permission, I'll give the order to cremate his remains," said Constantine. "Burial plots are running at a premium, and I imagine his funds will be tied up by the courts for some time."

"That will be fine," said Gold dryly. "I certainly wouldn't want to put a financial strain on the Vainmill Syndicate." He paused. "Have we anything further to discuss?"

"Just one thing."

"And what is that?"

"You are in possession of something that doesn't belong to you," said Constantine. "Since you seem disinclined to use it, I was wondering if you had any intention of returning it?"

"I don't know what you're talking about," said Gold coldly.

Constantine stared at him for a moment, then shrugged.

"Thank you for your time, Doctor Gold," he said at last. "I'm sure we will meet in person one of these days."

"I doubt it," replied Gold, breaking the connection.

He sat motionless for a few minutes, then got to his feet, commanded the door to open, and walked out into the living room, where Simon was seated on a high-backed chair, reading.

"I just heard from Richard Constantine," he announced.

"Oh?" said Simon, placing his book down on a table.

Gold nodded. "Kozinsky's dead."

"Well, that's hardly a surprise," replied his son. "Did he say anything else?"

"Not really," said Gold. "Oh, he asked me to return the video footage of the faeries' training session, but that was all."

"Oh," grunted Simon. He reached for his book.

"Doesn't that seem curious to you?" asked Gold.

"Curious?" repeated Simon. "In what way?"

"Why would he have taken the time to tell me Kozinsky was dead? He could easily have delegated the responsibility. And the only other thing he did was make a request that he knew I'd turn down. Why?"

"You're an important man," said Simon. "And,

more to the point, you're an important thorn in his side. Maybe he felt it was time to speak to you face to face."

"I don't think so," said Gold. "There has to be another reason."

"For instance?"

Gold shrugged. "I don't know. He didn't seem inclined to continue the conversation, so obviously he learned what he wanted to know. But for the life of me, I can't imagine what it was."

"Maybe he wanted to make sure that you hadn't told any other Jesus Pures about Kozinsky," suggested Simon. "I imagine Vainmill is scared to death that his little exploit will become public and that someone else will pick up the gauntlet, so to speak."

Gold shook his head. "He never mentioned it. And even if I had told anyone, it's hardly the kind of information I'd volunteer to him." He lowered his head in thought. "He never mentioned the incident with Titania, either. I wonder what he could have wanted."

"Titania?" repeated Simon. "You mean the Andrican female?"

"Yes."

"What incident?"

Gold looked uncomfortable. "A little misunderstanding aboard the *Comet*."

"You never mentioned it."

"It wasn't important."

"What happened?" persisted Simon.

"I'm afraid that I scared the living daylights out of her," admitted Gold.

Simon frowned. "Why?"

"I misinterpreted her actions, and she then misinterpreted mine. As I say, it was just a mis-understanding."

"What did you do to frighten her?"

"I thought she was flaunting her body for my benefit, so I yelled at her," said Gold uncomfortably.

"Are you sure you misinterpreted her actions?" said Simon. "After all, she *is* a prostitute. Perhaps the madam told her to do that in the hope of weakening your resolve."

"Weakening my resolve?" exploded Gold. "Do you think I had to *resolve* not to be tempted by her?"

"I meant that such an act might weaken your resolve about removing her from the *Comet*," said Simon carefully.

"I'm more determined now than ever," said Gold adamantly. "She can't begin to know the effect she has on human men."

"You might be overreacting. When all is said and done, she's an *alien*."

"A very erotic alien," responded Gold.

"No human could find her sexually attractive."

"Why not? In point of fact, she's quite attractive."

"I trust you're not speaking from personal experience."

"Remember whom you're speaking to!" snapped Gold.

Simon stared at his father. "What exactly *did* she do?" he asked at last.

"Nothing," said Gold. "I told you—it was a mis-understanding. The subject is closed."

Simon continued staring at him for another moment, then shrugged. "Whatever you say."

"*That's* what I say," replied Gold, aware that he should let the subject drop, but unwilling to let his son have the last word. He paused. "Anyway, Constantine never mentioned it."

"I'm sure that the customers scare the prostitutes all the time," suggested Simon. "After all, the people who frequent such places aren't exactly normal. Probably they go there supplied with whips and chains and the like."

A picture of Titania, arms and legs bound, flashed across Gold's mind. He couldn't decide whether he was horrified or fascinated by it.

"That's enough," he muttered at last, shaking his head in a physical attempt to eradicate the image. "Let's get back to the important question: why did he contact me personally?"

"I've already given you the most likely answer," said Simon.

Gold shook his head. "That's not good enough. There's got to be something more. He mentioned that he'd been trying to get through for a while, but that I hadn't answered his page. Why would a man who's in charge of such an enormous operation take two or three hours out of his day trying to tell me that Kozinsky was dead? The only unexpected news he could have given me would have been that Kozinsky was still alive."

"You're making a mystery out of a common courtesy," said Simon with certainty.

"Perhaps," said Gold. He tensed suddenly. "How long have you been here, Simon?"

"About half an hour."

"Where were you before that?"

"At my apartment. Why?"

"That's where Constantine contacted you before, isn't it? When he told you that Kozinsky was in the *Comet*'s hospital?"

"Yes."

"He could have spoken to you again, instead of trying to get through to me. Why didn't he?"

Simon shrugged. "I'm sure I don't know."

Gold smiled triumphantly. "Suddenly I'm sure that *I* do."

"Oh?"

"He didn't want to relay any information to me," said Gold. "We both knew Kozinsky couldn't last out the day. He just wanted to make sure I was at home.'

"Why?"

"I don't know—but it's got to have something to do with the *Comet*. And, more to the point, it has to have something to do with Constantine himself." He paused. "Put it all together and what do you get? That Constantine is going up to the *Comet*, and he wanted to make sure I wouldn't be there!"

"What difference could it possibly make to him?"

"I don't know—but it's important to him that I remain on Deluros, or he wouldn't have checked up on my whereabouts."

"Well, he's got his wish."

"Not for long," said Gold. "I want you to book me passage up to the *Comet* while I change into some fresh clothes."

"For what purpose?"

"I don't know yet," replied Gold. "But if he doesn't want me up there, then that's exactly where I belong. If he's afraid I can disrupt whatever it is that he's doing, then the very least I can do is try to make his fears come true."

"This is crazy!" protested Simon. "You've just come back from the *Comet*. He has no reason to assume that you have any intention of ever returning to it. If he was really going up there and didn't want you to follow him, the very last thing he would do would be to contact you in a manner that would arouse your suspicions."

"You think I'm wrong?" said Gold. "Fine. *I* think I'm right, and I'm going to act on my belief."

"You're getting to the point where you're spending more time up there than one of their customers," complained Simon.

Gold's entire body tensed, and for a moment Simon thought his father was about to take a swing at him. Then the moment passed, and Gold relaxed.

"All right," he said in clipped tones. "Arrange a shuttle for me, and—" He broke off in midsentence. "No, that won't do. Any shuttle that goes up to the *Comet* would probably forward a list of passengers so Security could run a financial check on them. Charter me a private ship; there's no sense letting Titania know I'm coming back up there."

"Titania?" said Simon, frowning.

"Did I say Titania?" replied Gold, surprised. "I meant the Steel Butterfly, of course." He fidgeted uneasily. "It's just that we had been talking about Titania ...."

His voice trailed off, and after an awkward silence he went off to shave, shower, and change his clothes.

Simon walked to Gold's office and arranged for his father's transportation up to the *Velvet Comet*. On the way back to the living room an unusual sound came to his ears, and he stopped until he could identify it.

It was Thomas Gold, absently humming a rhythmic alien melody as he stood before the bathroom mirror, combing his hair as meticulously as he ever did before appearing in front of a video camera.

10

Gold stood at the Security station in the *Velvet Comet*'s airlock. He had been standing there for almost five minutes.

Finally a burly man of medium height, with a thick shock of unruly black hair and a beard which was starting to turn gray, approached.

"All right," he said, walking up to one of the guards. "What's the problem?"

"It's Doctor Gold, sir," replied the green-clad woman. "I checked with the reservation desk, and he's not expected—and he refuses to tell me the purpose of his visit."

The burly man turned to Gold and stared at him, hands on hips.

"Twice in one day: this *is* a surprise," he said at last. "However, if you've changed your mind about Kozinsky's body, I'm afraid you're too late. He's already been cremated."

"I'm not here for Kozinsky."

"Then to what do we owe the pleasure of this unexpected visit, Doctor Gold?"

"I'm looking for Richard Constantine," responded Gold.

"Well, you're looking for him about four thousand miles too high up. He's in his office on Deluros VIII."

"I have reason to believe that he's aboard the *Comet*."

"You'll have to take my word for it that he's not here."

"And who are you?" demanded Gold.

"You can call me Attila. I'm the Chief of Security."

"I've heard of you," commented Gold. "At least, I remember your name."

"It was chosen to be remembered," replied Attila with some satisfaction. He paused. "I'm sorry you've wasted a trip, Doctor Gold."

"I don't know that I have," said Gold firmly. "I think he's up here."

"And I tell you he's not."

"I don't believe you."

"Well, there's no need to argue about it," said Attila reasonably, walking over to a computer bank. "We can contact him in his office right now."

Gold shook his head. "Computers can be rigged."

"What will it take to convince you, Doctor Gold?" asked Attila. "I'm not at liberty to show you every suite on the *Comet*, and from what I know of the Jesus Pures you wouldn't agree to look anyway."

"He's not in any of the suites," said Gold with conviction.

"Where do you think he is?"

"I'm not sure."

Attila scrutinized Gold's intense, ascetic face for a long minute. "If I didn't know that your religion forbids it, I'd say that you'd been drinking, Doctor

Gold. Do you know just how little sense you're making?"

"He's here," repeated Gold stubbornly. "And I'm not leaving until I see him."

"Then we'll move a bed into the airlock," said Attila. "Because I'm not letting you into the *Comet*."

"Tell the Steel Butterfly I'm here," said Gold. "She'll let me in."

Attila nodded to another green-uniformed Security man. "Fair enough, Doctor Gold. If she agrees to see you, I'll have you escorted to her office." He smiled. "Who knows? We might even find a companion for you."

"Keep a civil tongue in your head!" said Gold sharply.

"When I have the audacity to enter your church without prior notice or authorization, you can tell me that," replied Attila, the smile still on his lips but the amusement vanished from his eyes. "In the meantime, try to remember that you have no more business visiting me at my place of business than I have visiting you at yours. And *I* haven't been waging a campaign of hate and fear against you," he concluded.

The Security man, who had been speaking into a tiny communicator in low tones, suddenly looked up.

"She'll see him," he announced. "She says to take him to her office and she'll get there as soon as she can."

"Tell her to bring Constantine with her," said Gold.

"He's not aboard the ship, sir," replied the Security man.

"Any word about whether the good doctor is still to be invisible?" asked Attila.

"No, sir."

"Then I think we'll allow our patrons to see who has decided to pay us a visit."

"I'd prefer that you didn't," said Gold.

"I don't doubt it," replied Attila. "However, your stated ambition is to put Vainmill, and hence the *Comet*, out of business. That means you intend to put *me* out of business." He paused. "Therefore, I hope you'll understand if I fight back in any way I can."

"How will allowing the patrons to see you escorting me to the Steel Butterfly's office help your cause?" asked Gold.

"Oh, *I'm* not escorting you, Doctor Gold," said Attila with a smile. "I have pressing business elsewhere aboard the *Comet*."

"Then who is?" asked Gold, suddenly apprehensive.

"Titania, I think," replied Attila. He turned to the Security woman. "Page her."

"What's the purpose of this?" demanded Gold.

"The faeries have been the focus of your attacks on us," explained Attila. "I think it will be more beneficial to my cause than to yours if our patrons see her leading you into the brothel."

Gold stared at the Security chief, an inscrutable expression on his gaunt, angular face.

"Take it or leave it, Doctor Gold," said Attila firmly. "You go with her, or you leave the ship. There's no third alternative."

"Let's get on with it," said Gold.

"I'm glad you've decided to be a reasonable man," said Attila. He turned to the Security woman. "If she hasn't got her translator with her when she arrives, send her back for it. And make sure she knows she's taking him to the Steel Butterfly's office, and not to one of the suites."

The woman nodded, and Attila turned back to Gold.

"Just out of curiosity, why do you think Constantine is up here?"

"Assuaging your curiosity isn't my business," said Gold coldly.

Attila shrugged, started to say something, seemed to think better of it, and left the airlock.

A moment later Titania showed up, this time with her translating device. She froze when she saw Gold, and gave him a wide berth as she approached the Security woman.

"You paged me?" she said, and her translated voice, though definitely feminine, struck Gold as much too mature for her body.

"This is Doctor Thomas Gold. You are to escort him to the Steel Butterfly's office, and remain there with him until she arrives."

Titania looked apprehensively at Gold.

"How long will that be?" she asked.

The Security woman shrugged. "Five or ten minutes, I suppose. Why?"

"May we take the tram?"

"Why not? We don't care who sees him this time."

Titania asked another half-dozen questions, eyeing Gold nervously the whole time. Finally, when the Security woman's irritation became apparent, the little Andrican sighed and walked to the door.

"Please follow me, Doctor Gold," she said.

Gold fell into step behind her, walked out into the Mall, and soon reached the escalator that led down to the tramway. Titania, still noticeably frightened of him, timed her progress so that they were never alone, and they rode the tramcar to the brothel in total silence.

A few moments later they were in the reception foyer, and Gold was suddenly aware of the curious glances that were being cast in his direction. He pulled himself up to his full height and glared back at each onlooker in turn. Most of them dropped their eyes; a few didn't, and one of them—a government official from distant Altair III—grinned at him with vast amusement.

Titania, who had started off and then noticed that Gold wasn't following her, came back to him and took his hand. Once more he felt the electric thrill he had experienced earlier in the day, but this time he didn't jerk his hand back.

"This way, Doctor Gold," she said.

He nodded, and allowed her to lead him through the foyer and down a crowded corridor that passed by a number of restaurants and bars. He saw what seemed to be a huge casino off to his right, but Titania led him away from it, into a corridor with a large RESTRICTED sign posted on it. She released his hand the instant they were no longer surrounded by prostitutes and patrons, and walked past four doors, stopping at the fifth. She then deactivated her translator just long enough to trill four melodic notes, and walked into the room as the door slid back.

Gold followed her, barely clearing the doorway before the door closed again, and found himself in what was obviously the Steel Butterfly's office. Holographs of some two dozen women, the Steel Butterfly's predecessors, formed four neat rows on one of the walls. Human and alien artifacts were scattered carefully about the room, displayed on tables and wall shelves. To one side of the room, just opposite an artificial fireplace, were a pair of couches which faced each other across a ebon-and-chrome table, the surface of which was a computer screen. The far corner of the room had been given over to the Steel Butterfly's newest possession: a glowing electronic representation of the horserace, both animals sparkling and glowing as they lunged, sweating and straining, for the finish line. He noted with some amusement that in this particular rendition of the race, the big red colt that had so captivated her was the winner.

"May I get you something to drink?" asked Titania.

"A cup of tea, thank you," said Gold.

The faerie walked to the Steel Butterfly's wet bar, vanished behind it for a moment, and then reemerged.

"She doesn't have any tea," she said.

"Water, then," said Gold.

She walked behind the bar once more, poured him a glass of water, and carried it across the room to him.

"Thank you," said Gold.

"You're welcome."

He stared down at her.

"How old are you?" he asked.

"Thirty-four," she replied.

"Galactic standard years?" he said incredulously.

"Yes."

"I don't believe it!" He stared at her. "You look so *young*!"

She seemed to find that amusing, though her translated voice remained impassive. "I *am* young."

"I mean that you look like a child."

"I will live for almost two hundred years."

"I know. I've read all about Andricans. But I'm still surprised that you don't look more mature."

"This is the way I will look until I die." She paused. "I'm sorry that it displeases you."

"It doesn't displease me," said Gold. He paused awkwardly. "In fact, I think you're quite lovely."

She smiled with childlike delight. "Do you really?"

He stared at her intently. "Yes."

Suddenly the smile vanished. "Then why do you keep shouting at me?"

He sighed. "I don't mean to shout at you, Titania. I'm just upset that circumstances have forced you to work here."

"But I *like* working here."

"That's because you don't know any better."

"There is no place I would rather be," she said adamantly.

"I realize that your surroundings are luxurious," said Gold. "But surely you would prefer to do something other than spend every day copulating with lecherous, sinful men who pay for your favors."

"Why? I *like* meeting new people."

"But you don't have to like having sex with them!"

"Why shouldn't I like it? Men are *much* better lovers than Andricans." She smiled and made a quick, emphatic motion with her hands that he didn't understand.

Gold closed his eyes for a moment, then looked at her again.

"What do Andrican females do for a living?" he asked.

Titania shrugged contemptuously, as if their jobs were too trivial even to mention. "They don't get to wear clothes like *this*." She spread her arms to show off her translucent silver gown.

"Don't do that," said Gold, unable to tear his fascinated gaze from her nipples, which were clearly visible beneath the soft fabric.

"I think it's pretty," she said, turning around once with a sensual alien grace that belied her childlike face. "Don't you like it?"

"Yes, I like it," he said intently.

"Then what's wrong with it?"

"It's indecent!" he muttered.

He was sure she would laugh at him, but she didn't.

"It's *supposed* to be indecent," she explained, the flat electronic tones of the translator mirroring her seriousness. "The *Velvet Comet* is a brothel."

"Don't you understand that God disapproves of what you're doing?" he demanded.

"*Your* god might disapprove," she replied, with a total lack of concern. "*Mine* doesn't."

"There is only one God," he said sternly.

"Oh, no," she corrected him. "There's yours, and mine, and the Lodinites', and the Canphorites', and the Bolarians have three. And those are just the ones I know about."

"There is one God," Gold repeated.

"I would not say that to a Bolarian priest," she replied.

"There is one God, and He condemns the sinful to everlasting hell."

"How does he know who is sinful?"

"He is watching us."

She threw back her head and laughed so loudly that he could hear the trilling of her real voice as well as the translated laughter.

"He is very much like some of the *Comet*'s patrons!" she said at last.

"That's blasphemous!"

She paused for a moment, then asked: "Do you fear your god?"

"Of course."

"Then why do you devote your life to someone you fear?"

"I fear His strength and power, but I love His compassion."

"If you can love someone you fear, then why do you think it is wrong for me to make love to people I don't fear?" she asked, genuinely puzzled.

"This is ridiculous!" snapped Gold. "Why am I wasting my time arguing religion with you?"

She backed away from him quickly. "You're angry again."

He watched her, fascinated by the movement of her breasts and hips.

"I'm not angry, Titania," said Gold, trying to control his voice. "I like you, truly I do. More than you can possibly know," he added in a strained voice. Then he shook his head. "But I don't understand you."

"I don't understand you either, but it doesn't make me shout at you." She stared at him for a moment. "Everybody else wants to have sex with me. All you want to do is shout."

"That's not true."

"You *do* want to have sex with me?" she asked with a disarmingly innocent smile.

"No!"

"I'm very good," she said, and even the translated voice sounded enticing. "Everyone says I'm better than a human woman."

"Don't say that!"

"You see?" she said with a shrug. "Nothing makes you happy. I guess you must just be angry with everyone."

"I'm *not* angry!" Suddenly he took a deep breath and walked over to a chair. "I've got to calm myself," he muttered.

He sat down and pressed his fingers to his temples.

"Does your head hurt?" asked Titania, staring at him with a catlike curiosity.

"It will pass."

"Can I do anything to make you feel better?"

He stared at her for a long moment. "You can deactivate your translator and sing a song," he said slowly. "I would find that very restful."

"If you wish," she said.

"But you must never tell anyone that I requested it," he added sharply.

She nodded and trilled a brief answer, and Gold, with a growing sense of excitement, realized that the translating device was already off.

A moment later the room was filled with her alien music, each melodic tone sounding like the chime of ice on the finest crystal. Gold leaned back as she crooned her song, waiting for the tension to drain from his throbbing head and finding to his consternation that it had spread throughout his body as he watched her swaying in time to the music.

Suddenly the room became silent, and Titania activated her translator again.

"Did you like it?" she asked.

"Very much," whispered Gold.

"Shall I sing another song for you?"

"I think you'd better not," he said with an enormous effort of will.

"You didn't like it." Gold imagined that he could distinguish a sense of *hurt* in the translated voice.

"Yes, I did. Please believe me."

"Then I will sing another song."

Before he could protest again, she had turned off her translator and a new melody permeated the room. Gold closed his eyes, leaned his head back against the couch, and found himself humming along with her.

"That was very lovely," he said when she had concluded.

"You are very easy to please," she replied, activating the translator.

"Am I?"

"Yes."

He stared unblinking at her. "How easy?" he said softly.

She looked at his flushed face and rigid body, and suddenly a smile of comprehension crossed her face.

"*Very* easy."

"Why do you think so?"

She walked over and stood directly in front of him, her posture one of open invitation.

"Because my job is pleasing people."

Gold's hands began shaking again.

"How can you look so innocent and be so wanton?" he whispered.

"How innocent do I look?" she asked, her alien eyes wide with mock curiosity.

"Like a little girl."

"Would you like me to be *your* little girl?" she asked. "To reward when I'm good and punish when I'm bad?"

He tried to answer, but all that came out was an unintelligible concoction of sound.

"Can I call you Daddy?" she continued.

"Don't do this," he whispered.

"Don't do what, Daddy?" she asked, amused by his obvious torment.

"Don't flaunt yourself before me," he said. "I'm a moral, God-fearing man!"

"Then you'll have to punish me," she said, grinning. "Would you like to put me over your knee?"

"Yes," he breathed, then jumped to his feet. "No!" he shouted. "I'm Thomas Gold, and I cannot be led astray!"

"Then can't I be your little girl anymore?" she asked with mock regret.

"Don't toy with me like this!" he pleaded. "You're just a child! You can't know what you're doing!" He stopped in mid-tirade and stared, wild-eyed, at her. "God, but you're beautiful!" he whispered. He looked at her silver, feathery hair. "What does it feel like?" he asked.

He reached out to her, and felt an even stronger sensation than that which he had experienced earlier in the cargo area.

"You look so very innocent!" he whispered, stroking her hair and neck.

"There's not an awful lot that she's innocent *of*," said a sardonic voice from behind him.

Startled, he whirled around and found himself facing the Steel Butterfly.

"How long have you been there?" he demanded.

"I just came in."

He stared at her, momentarily disoriented.

"I—" He stopped, looked at the grinning Titania, then back at the madam. "I only . . . " He began stammering, and his voice trailed off.

"Titania, you can leave us now," said the Steel Butterfly.

The little faerie skipped across the room and out the door while Gold watched her, blinking furiously and struggling for composure.

"She tried to—" he began, then stopped again and stared at his hands, as if they were alien things that belonged to someone else. Finally he looked up at the Steel Butterfly. "All I did was touch her hair, I swear it!"

"I believe you."

"I was just curious as to how it felt," he continued, feeling like a fool but unable to make himself stop talking. "It's not like human hair, you know. Its texture is, well, different, and I wanted to touch it and see what it felt like, to see if it was more feathery or hairy, to the touch I mean. So I got up and I walked over and I reached out and I touched it. That's all I did. I'm Thomas Gold, and I would never do anything else, anything more. I just touched her hair. Just that, I swear to God!"

"Maybe you'd better take a minute to compose yourself, Doctor Gold," said the Steel Butterfly, walking to the bar and starting to mix herself a drink.

"I *am* composed," he said unsteadily.

"Perhaps not as much as you think," she replied without looking up.

He took a step toward her, felt a mild sense of discomfort, and suddenly became aware that he had an erection that was clearly visible beneath his trousers. He immediately sat down on the nearest chair.

"Don't look so distressed, Doctor Gold," said the Steel Butterfly, not without a trace of sympathy. "You're not exactly unique."

"I don't know what you mean."

"I mean that the business of a brothel is human frailty."

"I didn't molest her!" he protested.

"I know you didn't. If you had tried, Security would have been here on the double. There are three very well-camouflaged holo cameras in the office."

"Oh my God!" he breathed. "Do you mean that everything that happened here is on a holo disk somewhere?"

She nodded. "Of course."

"What right did you have to spy on me?" he demanded hotly.

"You're in *my* office, Doctor Gold," she replied. "I'd hardly consider it spying."

"You purposely stayed away while she flaunted herself at me!" he raged. "You set me up for this!"

The Steel Butterfly shook her head. "I did no such thing, Doctor Gold."

"Then why weren't you here to meet me when I got to the office?" he demanded.

"I was busy," she replied. "And I hardly expected to see you twice in one day," she added reasonably.

"Where's Constantine? This was *his* idea!"

"He's on Deluros VIII, I imagine," answered the Steel Butterfly.

"No!" yelled Gold. "He's here!"

"We're expecting him tomorrow, but I can attest to the fact that he's not aboard the *Comet* at this moment."

"Lies! All lies!"

"It's the truth."

"But he *must* be here!" persisted Gold, his voice suddenly confused and almost whining. "That's why I came—to see him."

"I think we both know why you came, Doctor Gold," she said gently.

"I only touched her hair!"

"What else would you have touched if I hadn't entered the room when I did?"

A look of utter panic flashed across his tortured face. "What do you intend to do with those holo disks?"

"I haven't thought about it," she replied.

"You mustn't show them to anyone!"

"Just a minute, Doctor Gold." She turned toward her tabletop computer terminal. "Cupid?"

"Yes?" said the computer's electronic voice.

"Put everything from the time Doctor Gold entered the office until he leaves into my Personal file." She turned back to Gold. "No one will be allowed access to what we say unless I order Cupid to release it." She paused. "You have certain disks of ours. Perhaps we could arrange a trade."

"Then I was right! This whole thing was your idea!"

"No, Doctor Gold. I didn't even know you were coming here. This whole thing was *your* idea!"

"How do I know you won't make copies first?"

She smiled. "How do I know *you* won't?"

He stared sullenly at her. "I won't part with them."

"Even in exchange for the record of what happened in here?"

"I have my reasons."

"I'm sure you do."

He stared at her, apprehension replacing outrage on his pale face.

"What happens now?"

"Nothing."

"What do you mean, nothing? Are you blackmailing me or aren't you?"

"Blackmail is an ugly word, Doctor Gold," said the Steel Butterfly. "I'm trying to effect a trade with you."

"I won't part with the Delvania disks!" he declared passionately.

"You absolutely insist on keeping them?"

"Yes!" he shouted, his eyes blazing in half-crazed defiance.

"You're the leader of more than two million Jesus Pures," she said pointedly. "Have you thought of the consequences if they should see this disk?"

"If that disk is ever released, I'll come back here and kill you with my own hands!"

She sighed. "You realize, of course, that your threat is now a matter of record?"

He looked confused. "But you told the computer . . . I thought you said that—"

"I said that no one could access this disk without my permission. That's valid only as long as I'm alive. Two minutes after you killed me Attila would be going through every disk in my Personal file, looking for a likely motive."

He began pacing the floor distractedly. "I'm sorry," he muttered. "I'm sorry. I said that in the heat of the moment. I couldn't kill anyone."

"I believe you."

"But I *can't* let my son see that disk!"

"And you won't trade the Delvanian disks to me?"

"I *can't!*"

She finished her drink and placed the empty glass on the bar.

"All right, Doctor Gold," she said. "My only concern is the *Velvet Comet*. The rest of Vainmill can go straight to hell for all I care." She paused. "If you'll promise not to mention the *Comet* or the faeries again in your broadcasts, I'll promise not to release the disk. You can go right on attacking Fiona Bradley and Vainmill to your heart's content, as long as you leave the *Comet* alone. Have we got a deal?"

"Yes."

"Then I guess that concludes our business," she said. "Do you need a few minutes before you leave?"

Suddenly exhausted, he nodded his head. "Thank you," he said wearily.

"You're welcome, Doctor Gold."

He spent a couple of minutes in silence, trying to control his alternating feelings of lust and shame, then got to his feet and followed her to the door.

She pointed to a nearby elevator.

"That leads to the service area. You're welcome to take it, if you'd like to get back to your ship without being seen."

"I think it would be best," said Gold. He turned to her, a puzzled expression on his face. "You're sure Richard Constantine isn't aboard the *Comet*?"

"You never really thought he was, did you?" she replied.

Thirty minutes later, as he sat in exquisite misery on the planet-bound ship, he still didn't know the answer to the Steel Butterfly's final question. Then the exertions of the long day caught up with him, and he nodded off to sleep.

The imp was waiting for him, as usual.

"Hi, Daddy," he said, and suddenly metamorphosed into a faerie in a translucent gown. "Did you bring me a present?"

"Yes, I did," said Gold. "But first you must close your eyes."

The faerie closed her eyes, her face a mask of happy anticipation, as Gold began slipping off his clothing.

"All right," he said after a moment. "You can look now."

"Oh, Daddy!" she crooned happily, her words a series of tinkling chimes.

11

"Attila wishes to speak to you on Channel K," announced Cupid.

"All right," said the Steel Butterfly. "Put him through."

The Security chief's holograph flickered into existence and took on shape and form.

"Got a minute to answer a couple of questions?" he asked her.

"For you? Always," she said pleasantly.

"Okay. First of all, what the hell is a Personal file?"

"Ah!" She smiled. "You've reviewed the disk."

"Didn't anyone ever tell you that if you want to maintain confidentiality you use a Priority file coded to your Vainmill Employee Number?"

"Of course," answered the Steel Butterfly. "But nobody ever told that to Doctor Gold."

"Then you just wanted him to *think* that Security couldn't access the disk?"

"Certainly," she said, amused. "You're slow today, Attila."

"I guess I must be," he admitted. "This Personal-file bullshit took me by surprise."

"You mentioned that you had two questions. What was the other?"

Attila's image stared directly at her for a moment, deadly serious.

"Who gave you the right to make a private treaty with Gold?" he said at last.

"You're referring to my promise never to make use of the disk, of course?" said the Steel Butterfly.

"*Your* promise," he said emphatically. "Not *mine*." He paused. "This disk is what we've been waiting for. We've finally got something that'll turn this man into a laughingstock, and you didn't even get him to turn over the Delvania footage for it."

"He'll never use what he got from Delvania," she said confidently.

"Maybe so, maybe not."

"I guarantee it."

"Even if you're right, that doesn't mean that someone else in his organization won't use it. For starters, he's supposed to have a son who's even more of a fanatic than *he* is."

"He'll never show it to his son."

"What makes you so sure?" persisted Attila.

"Because understanding sexual obsession is my business," replied the Steel Butterfly.

"Well, protecting the *Comet* is mine," answered Attila. "I'm going to have to turn that disk over to Constantine."

"You're a fool," she said. "Thomas Gold is no threat to anyone except Thomas Gold."

"That sounds impressive, but it doesn't mean shit if you're wrong. What if he attacks us again? After all, a fanatic doesn't have to honor his word."

"What if he does attack us again? He's been

doing it for months, and what good has it done him?"

"Are you saying that you *expect* him to break his bargain?"

"It's a possibility."

"And yet you don't consider him a danger to us?" he demanded incredulously.

"Let me put it another way," she said. "Where does your loyalty lie—to the *Comet* or to the Vainmill Syndicate?"

"They're the same thing."

She shook her head vigorously. "They're *not*. Vainmill was all set to shut us down before Fiona Bradley took over. We're just a tiny cog in one of their many machines."

"What are you getting at?" asked Attila, staring at her intently.

"I'm trying to tell you that Richard Constantine is a far greater threat to the *Velvet Comet* than that poor, guilt-ridden religious fanatic ever will be."

"Constantine?" said Attila with a sarcastic laugh. "Who the hell do you think has been fighting Gold for us?"

"Only because it's a good career move at this point in time," responded the Steel Butterfly. "It's his first assignment in Fiona Bradley's administration, and he wants to impress her. He'll have no compunction about cutting us loose the moment we become bothersome to him. He's so ambitious he makes Cassius look fat and full."

"Even if you're right, that's all the more reason to get rid of Gold by using that disk."

She shook her head again. "In his current mental and emotional state, he's the least effective foe we could have. Find some way to discredit him, and whoever replaces him will be far more formidable."

"Let me get this straight," said Attila. "You're telling me that you want Gold attacking us precisely because this obsession he's got for the faerie is driving him off the deep end?"

"That's right." She paused. "There are lots of jobs for Security men—but once you've been the madam of the *Velvet Comet*, no other position is acceptable. I intend to do whatever it takes to make sure that my job doesn't disappear out from under me."

He stared at her and sighed heavily. "And I thought *I* was a cold son of a bitch!"

She smiled patronizingly at him. "You're young yet. I still have hopes for you."

12

Gold looked up from his computer when he heard Simon knocking at the door.

"Yes?"

"They're here," said Simon.

"I'll be right out," said Gold, deactivating the computer. He stood up, took a few steps toward the door, and then hesitated.

"Simon?"

"Yes, Father?"

"I'm just finishing up some notes for one of my sermons. Tell them I'll be out in five minutes."

"All right."

Gold returned to the computer.

"Activate," he said.

The computer hummed to life.

"Bring up the last image."

A holograph of two nude female faeries, locked in a lesbian embrace, appeared directly above the computer.

He studied the image, his head beginning to throb again.

"Action."

The frozen faeries came to life, kissing and caressing one another under the direction of an offstage tutor.

"Deactivate in four minutes," said Gold, leaning forward and staring unblinking at the holograph.

The faeries rolled across their enormous bed, changing positions frequently, their actions more frenzied—and suddenly the computer shut down.

"What happened?" demanded Gold.

FOUR MINUTES HAVE ELAPSED.

Gold read the printed response and shook his head vigorously.

"It couldn't have been more than 30 seconds!"

I HAVE JUST RECHECKED MY FUNCTIONS. THERE HAS BEEN NO ERROR.

"There *must* have been!"

I HAVE CHECKED MY FUNCTIONS YET AGAIN, AND THEY ARE ALL WORKING PROPERLY.

Gold took his timepiece from his wrist and laid it down next to the computer.

"Show me the same footage again," he ordered.

The two faeries reappeared, passionately stroking and kissing each other precisely as they had done before.

Gold watched them intently, and even after the computer had deactivated he continued to stare at the empty space where they had appeared. As reality slowly impinged upon him, he sighed and leaned back on his chair, feeling mildly uncomfortable as the knotted muscles in his arms and legs began relaxing.

Suddenly he leaned forward and checked his timepiece. Seven minutes had elapsed.

"Damn!" he muttered. "Activate."

The computer came to life once more.

"Run it again."

Once again the two faeries appeared, and this time Gold made sure to check the time every few seconds. He was eighty-five seconds into the footage when Simon knocked on the door.

"What is it?" he snapped.

"Are you all right, Father?"

"Of course I'm all right! What do you want?"

"I thought you were coming out in five minutes. It's been almost fifteen."

"Five, fifteen—what's the difference? I'm busy!"

"Can't it wait?" asked Simon.

"No, it can't!"

"How much longer will you be?" persisted Simon.

"As long as it takes. Now leave me alone!"

There was no reply, and Gold walked back to the computer, which was still running the scene.

"Start it again," he commanded. "And put the running time above them."

The computer instantly complied, and Gold stared at the scene before him with renewed intensity. Finally it flickered out of existence.

"All right," he said grudgingly. "You were right. Deactivate."

He stood up, paused a moment until his breathing became more normal, and then left his office and walked to the living room, where his son, daughter, and grandson were waiting for him.

"Christina!" he said, smiling. "How wonderful it is to see you again!" He looked down at Jeremy. "My goodness! You've grown another inch! Are you ready for a trip to the museum tomorrow?"

Jeremy assured him that he was looking forward to it, then ran off to the dining room to help Corinne set the table.

Christina surveyed her father critically. "You've been under quite a strain," she remarked at last.

"Why should you think so?" asked Gold defensively. "I was just working on a sermon."

"I wasn't talking about that," she replied. "You've got to have lost fifteen pounds since the last time I was here."

"Maybe two or three," he said. "But hardly fifteen."

"Have you seen a doctor?" she continued. "You really don't look well, Father."

"I appreciate your concern, but I feel fine," he said.

"Well, you don't look it."

"I trust you intend to spend an equal amount of time nagging your mother about the weight she's gained," said Gold.

"*She* looks healthy. *You* don't."

"I told you—I'm fine."

"Simon, do *you* think he's all right?" she asked her brother worriedly.

"It's none of Simon's business," interrupted Gold. "Besides, he's got more important things to do these days than spend his time playing nursemaid to a perfectly healthy man."

"You mean his book?"

"That, too," said Gold. "But I've been letting him handle a lot of the church's routine administrative duties for the past few weeks while I work on my sermons." He paused. "I trust you heard the last two?"

"Of course."

"Did they sound as if they were given by a doddering old man with one foot in the grave?"

"No," she admitted. "But you must have used a lot of makeup and some very careful camera angles. You couldn't have lost all this weight since your last broadcast."

"I told you—you're exaggerating." He tried to change the subject again. "By the way, what did you think of them?"

"Them?"

"My sermons."

"They were fine," said Christina, deciding that any further discussion of her father's health would simply result in an argument. "Robert and I noticed that you haven't mentioned the Andricans at all for the past two weeks. Did Vainmill release them from their contracts?"

"No," said Gold, suddenly uncomfortable. "I just thought I'd do better to focus on Fiona Bradley for a while. After all, the faeries are just the symptom; Bradley and Vainmill are the disease."

"I suppose you're right," she said. "But after that video special last week about how the *Comet* has had to adapt to their needs, I was sure you'd be concentrating on them again.'

"They've pretty much served their purpose," said Gold. "We don't want the public getting tired of them."

"You make this sound more like a political campaign than a moral crusade," remarked Christina.

"To some extent it is precisely that," interjected Simon. "If we get the Andricans released, Vainmill will still be in the business of doing evil. But if we can bring Vainmill down, the Andrican situation will be resolved simultaneously."

"I never thought I'd hear Simon Gold equating politics and religion," she said with a smile.

"I'm not," said Simon stiffly. "But we're waging a battle to win men's souls, and it would be foolish not to use every weapon at our disposal."

"Mother mentioned one of those weapons," said Christina. "A man named Kozinsky, from the Declan system."

"Then I trust she also mentioned that we had nothing to do with it," answered Simon heatedly.

"She didn't *have* to mention it," she replied. "I know my father." She looked directly into Simon's eyes. "But I'll bet *you* had him condemned to eternal damnation before he had drawn his last breath."

"He tried to take human lives," said Simon.

"I notice you didn't say *innocent* human lives," she remarked, amused.

"Innocent or guilty, it makes no difference. The Lord tells us that we must not kill."

"I think that under the right circumstances, you could wipe out a regiment without turning a hair," she said.

"Christina, you shouldn't say that about your brother," said Gold. "He happens to be the most righteous man I've ever been privileged to know."

"That's just the kind of man who will commit any crime without compunction if he's convinced he's right," said Christina.

"I'm perfectly willing to be judged for my past and present sins," said Simon irritably. "But if it's all the same to you, I don't feel like defending myself for sins as yet uncommitted and unconceived."

"I didn't say you *would*, Simon," replied his sister. "Just that you *could*."

"Rubbish!"

"Not necessarily," commented Gold. "I suspect that anyone could commit *any* sin under the proper circumstances."

She shook her head. "Not you, Father," she said firmly.

"Even me."

"Thomas Gold? I doubt it."

"Then allow me to thank you for your vote of confidence, even while I disagree with it," he said ironically. "By the way, where's Robert?"

"He's arriving a few hours before your broadcast next Thursday evening."

Gold turned to Simon. "This animosity between you and your brother-in-law has got to stop. We're supposed to be a family, and I'm getting sick and tired of seeing each of you only when the other is absent. You're both mature adults; it seems to me that you ought to be able to get along with each other for an evening without arguing."

"I agree," said Simon.

"Then when are the two of you going to make an effort?" persisted Gold.

"We already have," replied Simon smugly. "In fact, I've been in contact with Robert twice within the past week."

"And you didn't fight?"

"Certainly not."

"I'm delighted to hear it," said Gold. "Surprised, but delighted."

"Robert's not totally unreasonable under the proper circumstances," added Simon.

"I've been trying to tell you that for years," said Christina.

"What's the cause of this new family harmony?" asked Gold.

"Your next broadcast, as a matter of fact," replied Simon.

"I'm afraid I don't follow you."

"I've got a surprise for you, Father," said Simon, looking inordinately pleased with himself.

"Can you tell me now, or do I have to wait until Thursday evening?" asked Gold.

"The sooner you know, the better, since I have a feeling that you're going to want to change your sermon."

"Change it?" repeated Gold. "What do you mean?"

"I assume you had planned to attack Fiona Bradley again?"

Gold nodded. "I'll be discussing Vainmill's abuse of aliens in the Bellermaine system."

Simon smiled and shook his head. "No you won't." He paused for dramatic effect. "You'll be talking about the Andricans."

"No," said Gold firmly. "I made them the subject of four broadcasts in a row. It's time to move on to other things."

"Not just yet," said Simon, still smiling.

"I won't talk about the faeries again. I made a promise."

"A promise?" asked Christina.

"To myself," answered Gold hastily.

"Well, you're about to break it," said Simon.

"No, I'm not," said Gold decisively. "The subject is closed." He paused. "Now, what's this surprise you've cooked up?"

"Robert is bringing two Andricans to Deluros with him," said Simon.

"*What?*"

"I thought we ought to do something to counter any favorable impression that Constantine's documentary created. You know, bring the faeries out and let them stand on the stage with you, so people can see just how inoffensive and vulnerable they are, maybe even have them say a few words about how prostitution is unknown on their home planet and what a terrible fate has befallen the Andricans on the *Velvet Comet*."

"Robert's bringing faeries to Deluros?" said Gold, blinking rapidly and trying to assimilate what he had just heard.

"He *is* an alien anthropologist, as well as an exobiologist," answered Simon. "He's had contact with races all over the galaxy. So when I got the idea while watching the documentary, I contacted him to see if it was feasible. He had to contact their government to see if he could get two of them to agree to come to Deluros with him, which is why I didn't know that we could actually accomplish it until yesterday." He paused. "I thought you'd figure it out when Christina showed up."

"Christina visits us every six or seven months," said Gold distractedly.

"But it's only been a month and a half since I was here," Christina interjected.

Gold stared at her, trying vainly to get his thoughts and emotions back into focus. "A month and a half?" he repeated disbelievingly.

She studied his face with concerned eyes.

"Are you all right Father?" she asked. "You look quite pale."

"I'm fine," he said, regaining his composure. "It's just that so much has happened in the last few weeks . . . ."

"Anyway, I thought you'd be pleased," continued Simon doggedly. "It's the opportunity of a lifetime to show the people a *real* Andrican, not one of those obscene *things* that have been trained by the Steel Butterfly and told what to say to the camera by Richard Constantine."

"But I promised . . ." muttered Gold.

"Well, obviously this isn't the surprise I had

hoped it would be," said Simon, making no attempt to hide his disappointment. "Still, I need a decision from you. If you think it's a bad idea, I'll have to get in touch with Robert immediately."

"Why?" demanded Gold, suddenly tense.

"There's no sense bringing the Andricans here without a reason," explained Simon. "If you really don't want to use them, I'll have Robert return them to their planet."

"Return them?" repeated Gold. "Return them?"

Simon's face clouded with concern. "Would you like to sit down, Father? Christina's right—you don't look at all well."

"You're not returning anything!" said Gold.

"Then you *do* want to use them?" said Simon, his enthusiasm returning.

"Definitely!" said Gold, his face suddenly alive with an excitement that Simon and Christina both misinterpreted. "I'm sorry if I seemed unappreciative at first, but I've had a lot on my mind lately." He laid a hand on Simon's shoulder. "It's an excellent idea; I should have thought of it myself. Now how about some dinner? I'm suddenly very hungry!"

They spent the next hour eating, and talking about Corinne's latest needlepoint, and Jeremy's schooling, and Robert's proposed fieldwork on the Outer Frontier, and then Gold excused himself, explaining that he had to work on his new sermon.

"That's the happiest I've seen him in months," remarked Simon.

"I thought he needed a rest," replied Christina. "I guess what he really needed was a new challenge." She paused and shook her head wonderingly. "He's a truly remarkable man."

And, thirty feet away, locked in his office, Thomas Gold stared transfixed, as the two female faeries once again went through their sexual contortions with a sensual alien grace.

13

The Steel Butterfly sat on a couch opposite her tabletop computer, a mixed drink in her hand.

Attila approached her door, waited for his retina pattern to register, and then entered the office as the door slid back into the wall.

"Good afternoon," she said as the door closed behind him and he approached her. "Thank you for coming so promptly."

"Happy to," he said. "And now that I'm here, maybe you'll tell me what's so important that you couldn't discuss it over the intercom."

"Richard Constantine is due to communicate with me in the next few minutes," she replied. "I thought you might find it interesting."

"That's what this is all about?" demanded Attila. "He calls you all the time."

"But this time he's got a crisis on his hands," she replied.

"What kind of crisis?"

"Thomas Gold's son-in-law is on his way to Deluros with a pair of faeries." She smiled. "I'm

176

not supposed to know it—but I am not without my sources inside Vainmill."

Attilla shook his head. "He's really gone over the edge, hasn't he?" he remarked. "Imagine importing his own prostitutes!"

She shook her head. "They're not prostitutes."

Attila frowned. "Then I don't understand."

"My guess is that he's going to use them on his next broadcast."

"So much for keeping his word." He paused. "What does this have to do with me?"

"You still haven't turned that disk over to Constantine. I thought you might like to see what he's like under pressure before you do."

"Why don't I just listen in from Security headquarters?" asked Attila. "He knows all your communications are monitored and logged."

"Because I'll want to discuss the conversation with you in private once it's over."

"Nothing that goes on in this place is ever in private," said Attila. "That's how we got the material on Gold in the first place."

"But you and I are going to put this whole conversation in a Priority file—what we say to Constantine, and what we say to each other after it's over. I've already instructed Cupid to do so."

"Do you really think all this secrecy is necessary?" he asked dubiously.

"Yes."

He stared at her. "You don't think a hell of a lot of Constantine, do you?"

"On the contrary, I think he's a very accomplished troubleshooter. Fiona Bradley's been using him for years, and he hasn't let her down yet."

"But?"

"But his loyalties are to Vainmill, and mine are

to the *Comet.* There's no question in my mind that sooner or later he can destroy Thomas Gold with or without our help—on the assumption that Gold doesn't self-destruct before Constantine goes to work on him—but I have a feeling that once Gold is out of the way, he'll get rid of the *Comet* as quickly and efficiently as possible before it can become a source of further embarrassment to Vainmill. After all, we're a more visible target than anything else in Entertainment and Leisure."

"Do you mind if I fix myself a drink?" asked Attila.

"I think you'd better not," she replied. "It doesn't bother *me*, but I have a feeling Constantine isn't going to want to see our Security chief with a drink in his hand."

"I notice that *you're* drinking," said Attila, sitting down on the opposite couch.

"It goes with the image," she replied. "Madams can drink. Security chiefs can't."

"I think I'll have to be a madam next time around," Attila remarked wryly. "By the way, how soon are you expecting this call?"

She checked her timepiece. "About three minutes."

"What did he do—have one of his secretaries tell you to be here waiting for it?"

She nodded. "He's a fanatic for punctuality."

They spent the next couple of minutes discussing additions to the Proscribed List—those patrons who had behaved so badly, either by abusing the prostitutes or cheating in the casino, that their presence aboard the *Comet* would not be accepted in the future—and then Cupid's voice interrupted them.

"Richard Constantine is attempting to make contact," announced the computer.

"Put him through," said the Steel Butterfly, turning to face Constantine's image above her tabletop.

"Good afternoon," he said to her, then turned to face Attila. "I wasn't expecting *you*," he added.

"I can leave if you wish," offered Attila.

He shook his head briskly. "It doesn't make any difference." His image turned back to the Steel Butterfly. "I have some interesting news for you."

"Oh?" she said noncommittally.

He nodded. "It seems that our documentary on the faeries is having some very beneficial side effects. Not only was it the highest-rated video of the month, but one of the major networks has made us a substantial offer for the rights to set a fictional drama aboard the *Comet*."

She frowned. "You mean they want to make holos of their performers up here?"

"No. They'll recreate portions of the *Comet* in a studio. But they'll be sending some scriptwriters and executives up in the next week to get a firsthand look at the ship. I'll have a list of their names sent up to you." He paused. "I want them afforded *every* courtesy. Vainmill will pick up the tab for it. Do I make myself clear?"

"Perfectly," replied the Steel Butterfly. "What type of show will they be doing?"

"Something mindless, no doubt," said Constantine. "It doesn't make any difference. The publicity can only do us good—and we *need* some good publicity," he added seriously. "I just got word that Thomas Gold's son-in-law, Robert Gilbert, is heading toward Deluros VIII with a couple of Andricans in tow. I had one of my assistants check his flight schedule, and he's due to land late Thursday afternoon. I can't imagine that Gold won't find some way to use them in his Thursday-night broadcast. Now I know why he hasn't mentioned the Andricans for the past two weeks; he was waiting for his son-in-law to arrive with the faeries." He paused. "I expect to hear from him any moment."

"From Gold?"

Constantine nodded. "I imagine he'll offer to forgo using the Andricans in exchange for our releasing our own faeries from their contracts."

"Which we won't do, of course," said the Steel Butterfly.

"They stay on the ship no matter what," said Constantine firmly. "I'm not going to let some half-baked religious fanatic get away with blackmailing me. If I gave in, there'd be no end to it." He looked at the madam and then the Security chief. "I've only actually spoken to him once, via computer, whereas you two have spent some time in his company. What was he like?"

"Pretty much like he appears in his broadcasts," offered Attila. "Rigid, austere, formal."

"I heard from Fiona Bradley that he made a bet on the horserace with Gustave Plaga when he was up there. How much was it for?"

"One credit," said the Steel Butterfly.

He frowned. "I was afraid of that." Constantine paused. "What about Kozinsky?" he asked suddenly. "Did you get the feeling that they knew each other?"

"I'm quite certain they didn't."

Constantine shrugged. "I didn't really want to use him anyway. There's no sense in alarming your patrons, or letting them think that they were ever in any physical danger. No, I need something on Gold himself."

"You're certainly in a better position to obtain it

than we are," she said. "After all, he's been aboard the *Comet* for a total of less than ten hours, and he was always either in my company or that of one or more Vainmill executives. He couldn't have done anything incriminating even if he had wanted to."

"When you were alone with him, what did he say to you?"

She smiled. "That was more than a month ago, and I must confess that I was far more concerned with what was going on in your executive meeting. I seem to remember that he was very uneasy about being here, and incensed by some of the things that he saw—but if you want something more specific than that, I'm afraid I can't help you." She paused. "We can pull the Security disks out and review them, if you'd like."

"I'll let you know at such time as I think it's necessary," said Constantine. He straightened some papers on his desk, then looked up. "What do you think made him decide to make the Andricans the focal point of his campaign?"

"They're aliens, and he's spent most of his career fighting against the exploitation of aliens."

"You're sure there was nothing more to it than that?" asked Constantine.

"Such as what?" she asked, surprised that he was so close to the truth with so little information.

"This may sound distinctly odd to you," he said, "but it occurs to me that if he found them sexually attractive he'd probably behave in precisely the same way. It might even explain why he hasn't released the Delvania material—maybe he doesn't want to share his private fantasies with anyone else." He paused, considering the notion. "Did he ever give you any indication that he might want to hop into bed with one of them himself?"

She shot a quick glance at Attila, then looked back at Constantine's holograph. "No, he didn't."

"Too bad," muttered Constantine. He sighed. "Well, it was a thought." He paused. "I may wind up using Kozinsky after all."

"I think the publicity could do us considerable damage," said Attila.

"Vainmill can weather it, never fear," replied Constantine. "The operative question is: could it do Gold even more damage than it does to us?" He straightened up in his chair. "Well, I'll have to explore the possibilities and come to a decison. In the meantime, hold a few of your best suites open starting about a week from now; I'll let you know the exact day the network people are due as soon as I find out myself."

He broke the connection.

"Well?" said the Steel Butterfly, turning to Attila.

"He's pretty sharp," said Attila. "He came awfully close to guessing the truth."

"What about the man himself?" she persisted.

"You were right about him," replied the Security chief. "It was '*Vainmill* can stand the damage' and '*I* won't be blackmailed.' There was nothing about the *Comet* at all. He'd sell us out in two seconds flat if he thought it would help him get rid of Gold." He stared at her. "You realize that we're in one hell of a lot of trouble. Not mentioning the disk prior to Constantine's call was one thing; denying we knew anything damaging about Gold in response to a direct question from our superior is another."

"What do you want to do about it?" she asked carefully.

He sighed. "If you and I decide the time has come to use what we've got, we will," he said at last. "But I agree with you: Richard Constantine is more of a threat to the *Comet's* existence than Thomas Gold."

"Then let's address ouselves to the disk. Cupid won't let us erase it; he's got a primary directive to protect his data's integrity. What do we do if Constantine actually does decide to study Gold's actions aboard the ship?"

"I can't erase it," agreed Attila, "but I can code it and hide it so well that they can't find it for months, even if they know what they're looking for. After all, the stuff we want to keep from them only takes up about ten minutes. Maybe I can even make an edited copy and put it where they *will* find it." He walked over to the bar and finally poured himself a drink. "What do you think he'll wind up doing about Gold's broadcast?"

"Nothing."

"I don't know," said Attila dubiously. "He's got to be under a lot of pressure to contain this situation."

"He's not a stupid man. If there was a way of shutting Gold up, he'd have come up with it before now. My guess is that he'll wait to see what Gold says before he makes a move."

"Who knows?" said Attila, downing his drink in a single swallow. "Maybe he won't have to do anything at all. Maybe Gold will take him off the hook by grabbing one of the faeries right in front of ten million viewers."

"It's a possibility," she agreed.

Attila looked surprised. "I was just joking," he said.

"I wasn't," answered the Steel Butterfly.

14

"I had no idea the auditorium was so large," remarked Robert Gilbert as he followed Christina and Simon down the long aisle to their seats, which were in a roped-off area reserved for VIPs and Gold's family. The huge stage, surrounded by half a dozen audio and holographic technicians, was currently occupied by two of Gold's subordinates, who were leading the enormous congregation in prayer.

"Ordinarily we use a much smaller one," answered Simon. "But given the importance of this broadcast, I decided to arrange for the biggest building we could get."

"I don't know if that was such a good idea," said Robert, frowning.

"Certainly it was," said Simon confidently. "Father has been working around the clock on this sermon. He's barely emerged long enough to eat."

"I wasn't referring to your father," said Robert. "I was thinking about the Andricans."

"What about them?" asked Simon as the three of them finally reached their seats.

"They're not used to crowds like this."

It was Simon's turn to frown. "You should have told me earlier."

"I didn't know what kind of facility you were using until five minutes ago," answered Robert.

"Why don't both of you calm down?" said Christina. "Father's not nervous, so why should you be? If the faeries are upset or frightened, he'll find some way to reassure them and calm them down, just the way he always used to do for Simon and me when *we* were afraid of something."

"I hope you're right," said Robert.

"I am," she replied firmly. "So just relax, and prepare to watch the beginning of the end of the Vainmill Syndicate."

Robert stared at her for a moment.

"You don't seriously believe anything he says tonight is going to bring Fiona Bradley's little empire crumbling down, do you?"

"If *you* didn't think so, why did you agree to bring the Andricans?" demanded Simon.

"Because I hoped it might help gain the *Velvet Comet's* Andricans their freedom. I'll be happy to settle for just that and nothing more."

"It will," said Simon decisively.

"Maybe," answered Robert. "But there's an awfully big difference between getting two aliens released from involuntary servitude aboard the *Comet* and destroying the biggest financial empire in the Republic."

"We'll dismantle it stone by stone," said Simon. "This is just the first step."

"If you say so," replied Robert, obviously unconvinced. He turned to Christina. "I think I'd better check on the Andricans. I left them with one of my assistants. I don't even know if they're here yet."

"Relax, Robert," said Christina soothingly. "Of course they're here. If they weren't you'd have been notified."

"I suppose so," he said uneasily. "But I think I'd better go backstage anyway, and let them know what they're in for. I told them they'd probably be in a holo studio with an audience of a couple hundred or so."

"Will you really feel better if you talk to them?" asked Christina resignedly.

"Yes, I will," he said, getting to his feet and walking up to an usher, who listened to him for a moment, then nodded his head and led him to a door marked NO ENTRANCE in the corner of the immense auditorium.

"He seems very nervous tonight," remarked Simon to his sister.

"He's worried about the faeries. He feels responsible for them."

"I hope he gets back before Father begins speaking."

"How soon is he due to begin?" asked Christina.

Simon checked his timepiece. "About five minutes."

"I'm sure he'll be back by then." She paused. "You know, I think he's only heard Father in person two or three times; we've spent most of our married life out among alien civilizations. I hope this particular sermon lives up to its advance billing."

"It will," Simon assured her. "I've never seen Father so absorbed before."

Gold's subordinates finished and left the stage, and the audience began conversing in low whispers while the holo technicians made their final sound and lighting checks.

"Where's Robert?" muttered Simon, staring at the NO ENTRANCE sign. "If he doesn't hurry, he's going to miss the beginning."

"He'll be here," said Christina.

"He'd better be," said Simon. "I'm sure Father will notice if he's missing, and I don't want anything to disturb him tonight."

"I told you, he'll—" She broke off as Robert came back through the doorway, looked around for a moment, got his bearings, and began walking toward them. "Satisfied?" she whispered triumphantly.

Simon grunted an acquiescence, and a moment later Robert took his seat.

"How are they?" asked Christina.

"Nervous," he replied. "I think they'll be all right, though."

"Why shouldn't they be?" asked Simon.

"They don't know what's expected of them. They just arrived ten or fifteen minutes ago, and your father hasn't briefed them yet."

"Stop fretting," said Christina. "Everything will be just fine."

Before Robert could answer, Thomas Gold, carrying a leather-bound Bible under his left arm, walked out onto the stage, and the audience suddenly fell silent.

"My God, he looks awful!" whisperd Robert, staring at his gaunt, black-clad father-in-law.

"Be quiet!" hissed Simon, glaring at Robert for a moment before turning back to watch his father.

"Good evening," said Gold in his rich baritone voice. "I'm very pleased to see that so many of you could be here with me tonight."

He looked out at the audience until his gaze fell on Christina, Robert, and Simon. He smiled at them, then looked back into the center camera.

"Ordinarily I'd begin this sermon as I have begun so many others," said Gold, "with a parable from the Bible. It's an old and time-honored method of propounding a moral position which can then be applied to a present problem. Ordinarily I would borrow from the words of Jesus, and show how they apply to each and every one of us." He held the Bible up. "Ordinarily I would bring the collective wisdom of this book to bear on my subject matter."

He paused, and glared into the camera.

"But that presupposes that the perpetrators of evil have read the Bible, that they haven't traded it in for a business ledger." He looked out over the audience again. "I don't have to quote the Bible to *you*," he continued. "You read it every day, and believe implicitly in its moral precepts." He paused. "What, then, am I to do? Shall I force my way into the corporate offices of the Vainmill Syndicate or the sin-filled bedrooms of the *Velvet Comet*, Bible in hand, demanding that they listen to me?" He shook his head regretfully, and sighed deeply. "Well, to tell you the truth, I'd do just that, if I thought it would do any good. But the simple fact that the *Velvet Comet* continues to hold its Andrican slaves in bondage is ample proof that nobody connected with that ship of shame has the slightest acquaintance with the Bible."

Gold fell silent for a moment, as if considering his next statement.

"But the fact that Vainmill and the *Velvet Comet* continue to ignore the teachings of the Good Book doesn't mean that we, in turn, have to ignore

Vainmill and the *Velvet Comet*," he went on. "They may turn their back upon the Word, but we will not reciprocate and turn a blind eye upon their evil practices. They may seek the darkness, but we shall continue to turn the light of the Lord upon them. They can deny, but the truth will seek them out."

"He's rambling a bit," whispered Robert.

"I haven't noticed it," replied Christina defensively.

Gold continued speaking, working himself into a rage over Vainmill's abuses of the Andricans without explicity identifying those abuses, drawing out each metaphor interminably.

"Brilliant!" murmured Simon. "Brilliant!"

Robert merely leaned forward on his chair and continued listening.

"For weeks I have spoken about these poor enslaved creatures," Gold was saying. "No, not creatures," he amended quickly, "but sentient beings as intelligent as you or I." He frowned. "You or *me*," he corrected himself. He stopped as if momentarily confused, then continued: "I've spoken about them, and lectured you about them, and talked about them—but up until now you haven't had the opportunity to see one of them with your own eyes. You haven't seen the vulnerability, or the compassion, or the—" he searched for the right word "—the *humanity* of these fellow beings. You haven't heard them." He stopped abruptly. "Oh, yes, you've heard *some* of them, two of them in fact—that is, you heard them if you watched what was ludicrously called a documentary that was broadcast a few weeks ago. But what you heard were carefully written, carefully rehearsed comments from two Andricans who were forced into appearing in the so-called documentary."

"How long did you say he worked on this sermon?" asked Robert, frowning.

"Constantly for the past four days," answered Christina.

"Well, you sure can't prove it by me," said Robert. "What's the matter with him? He's rambling and digressing and using the wrong words, and his delivery is—"

"Hush!" snapped Simon.

"So tonight I am going to introduce you to a pair of *real* Andricans," Gold continued. "You're going to see just what we've been talking about—what *I've* been talking about. You're going hear their comments." He stopped again. "Of course, you know I mean their *translated* comments. And unlike the carefully scripted mock documentary that Vainmill foisted upon the public, this documentary—this *sermon*—is totally unrehearsed. I have never seen or spoken to these two Andricans, or indeed to *any* Andricans except for the poor imprisoned creatures who have been forced to work aboard the *Velvet Comet*." He turned and nodded to someone who was standing in the wings, and a moment later the two faeries, one male and one female, walked slowly, timorously, out onto the stage.

Gold watched them intently as the camera followed their progress. Finally they came to a halt about six feet from him, looking very uneasy, and stared up at him. He remained motionless, almost catatonic, for the better part of a minute. Finally the nearest cameraman's wild gesticulations caught his attention, and he suddenly remembered his audience.

"You see how small they are," he said. "How

frail and defenseless, how tiny and vulnerable, how childlike and innocent."

He went on, his speech broken by awkward pauses, describing in profuse detail what the audience could plainly see for itself. Then came the interview, which was even more disjointed.

"What's the matter with him?" whispered Robert, his voice filled with concern. "He's white as a ghost."

"His hands are shaking, too," noted Christina. She turned to her brother. "He's ill, Simon. We should never have let him go through with this."

"He'll come through it all right!" whispered Simon furiously. "His timing's a little off, that's all."

"He looks like he's going to collapse any minute, and all you can say is that his timing's a little off?" demanded Robert.

"He's Thomas Gold!" repeated Simon, more to himself than to Robert. "He's Thomas Gold, and nothing can stop him from delivering the Word and smiting down his enemies!"

He turned back to the stage and stared intently at his father, as if he could force an end to the broken sentences and agonizing pauses by the sheer force of his will.

Gold continued speaking with the faeries for another three minutes, then ushered them offstage and returned to face his audience.

He stared at them, his eyes unfocused, for a long minute. Then he drew himself up to his full height, cleared his throat, and began speaking.

"It is said that the meek will inherit the Earth. Certainly no race can be said to be meeker . . . more meek . . . than the Andricans, and they have no desire to inherit the Earth. All they want is to live in peace and freedom on their own planet. And yet two among them . . ."

He spoke on and on, and suddenly, after another lengthy pause, he seemed to pull his thoughts together. The last five minutes of his sermon constituted a harsh and well-reasoned attack on the *Velvet Comet*. There were only ten Commandments, he pointed out, ten moral laws from which all human jurisprudence and social custom had derived. One by one he went throught them, pointing out in outraged detail how the *Comet* had either broken them or led its misguided clientele into breaking them. He concluded with a righteous demand that Vainmill release the Andricans immediately.

"Well?" asked Robert, turning to Christina.

"He's not himself," she said.

"I just don't know," answered Robert. "I would have agreed with you right up to the point when the Andricans left the stage, but those last few minutes were like the Thomas Gold of old. His voice was strong, his gestures were right, he had the audience eating out of the palm of his hand. If he can think on his feet like that, maybe he's not as sick as I thought. Maybe he just had an off night."

There was a momentary silence, and they became uncomfortably aware of thousands of voices whispering the very same doubts about Gold's physical condition.

"He didn't think on his feet," Simon said finally, his expression puzzled. "He *remembered* on his feet."

"I don't think I understand you," said Robert.

"That discourse on the Ten Commandments," answered Simon. "He gave the same sermon, word for word, about six years ago. It wasn't directed at the *Comet*, of course—he was attacking the Quantrell Conglomerate just after they had broken the miners' strike on Brazos II—but except for that, it was identical."

"If he wandered aimlessly for the first twenty-five minutes, and pulled the final five minutes out of an old sermon, then what was he working on all week long?" asked Robert, puzzled.

"I don't know," answered Simon, his voice troubled. "I really don't know."

"What difference does it make?" said Christina. "Both of you are missing the point. He's overworked to the point of exhaustion. Make any excuse you want, Simon, but he's never sounded like this before."

"He didn't sound overworked at the end," said Simon stubbornly. "He sounded just like he always does."

"You're deluding yourself, Simon," she said, her voice heavy with concern. "Haven't you looked at him? He's lost almost twenty pounds, the color is gone from his face, and his hands never stop shaking. And don't tell me he was just nervous or upset tonight, because we've both been with him all week. Haven't you noticed how he'll start to say something and then just stare off into space with a strange look on his face? He's sick, Simon, and he needs help!"

Robert became uncomfortably aware of the attention they had been attracting.

"This is neither the time nor the place to discuss it," he said firmly. "Let's get him and take him back home."

"I agree," said Simon, staring back at the closest group of onlookers until they uncomfortably began averting their eyes.

"Wait until the crowd finishes filing out," said Christina. "The last thing he needs now is to have some of them come up and ask him what went wrong tonight."

Robert nodded, and the three of them waited in silence for another ten minutes until the last few stragglers, convinced that they wouldn't get a chance to see Gold again, were walking up the long aisles toward the exits. Then they got up and walked to the NO ENTRANCE sign. When the guard recognized Simon he stepped aside and allowed them to pass.

Simon led them down a corridor, took a right turn, and stopped in front of a door.

"Father, are you ready to leave?" he said.

There was no answer.

"Father?" said Simon, knocking loudly on the door.

There was still no response from within, and finally Simon pressed his thumb against a small computer. It took about three seconds to register his thumbprint, and then the door slid open.

"It's empty," said Robert, stepping inside and looking around.

"How about the bathroom?" asked Christina.

Robert walked across the room and looked into the small lavatory, then turned to her and shook his head. "He's not here."

"Then where can he be?" asked Simon.

"Let's check the Andricans' room," suggested Robert. "Maybe he's with them."

"Where is it?" asked Simon.

"Follow me," said Robert, leading them out into the hall.

He retraced his steps to the point where they

had turned, and then followed the original corridor about fifty feet.

The sound of staccato, atonal trilling came to their ears.

"What's that?" asked Simon.

Robert frowned. "An Andrican."

"Are you sure?" asked Christina. "Father said they sounded melodic."

"Usually they do," said Robert, allowing the computer to read his thumbprint.

The door slid open, and they saw Gold, his cheek and forehead red with blood, struggling with one of the Andricans.

"Father!" exclaimed Simon.

Gold looked at the door with wild eyes and shouted something unintelligible.

Robert instantly commanded the door to close.

"What are you doing?" demanded Simon. "They're attacking him!"

Robert turned to Christina, who had an expression of dawning horror on her face.

"Take your brother home," he ordered her. "I'll bring your father along later."

"Open the door!" screamed Simon. "They're killing my father!"

"Nobody's killing anyone," said Robert. "I want you to go home with Christina. I'll take care of this."

They suddenly heard more frantic trilling and another yell from Gold.

Simon tried to push Robert away from the door.

"Let me in, damn you!" he raged.

"Aliens are my business," said Robert firmly. "Now go away and let me handle them."

"That's my father in there!"

"Simon, I'm bigger that you and stronger than

you, and I'm not going to open this door until you leave." He stared levelly at his brother-in-law. "And if you're still standing here in five seconds I'm going to break your jaw."

Something in the tone of Robert's voice convinced Simon that he was in earnest, and he stared at him unbelievingly.

"Come, Simon," said Christina. "It's all right. Father's not in any danger, truly he's not. Robert will take care of everything."

"But—"

"Simon!" she said urgently, pulling at his arm.

Simon made a rush for the door, and Robert drove a fist into his stomach. He groaned and doubled over, gasping for breath.

"Now get him out of here!" ordered Robert.

Christina nodded, and Simon, still gasping, struggled weakly but finally allowed himself to be led away.

Robert waited until they were out of the corridor, then opened the door again and took in the scene at a glance. His assistant was sprawled out on the floor, semiconscious from a blow to the head that Gold had evidently delivered with a heavy makeup jar that lay a few inches away from him. One of the Andricans, the female, crouched terrified in a corner, while Gold was struggling to rip the clothing from the male.

"Go away!" screamed Gold when he saw Robert.

"Let him go," said Robert gently, as he approached Gold carefully.

"Leave us alone!"

Gold took a swing at Robert when he came within reach. Robert ducked, and the faerie twisted loose and raced across the room. Gold began chasing him, but Robert, younger and faster, managed to position himself between them.

"I'm not going to let you touch him again," said Robert calmly. "Now, I want you to go to the other side of the room and try to compose yourself."

Gold uttered a guttural snarl and launched himself at Robert, who sidestepped his charge and encircled him with his arms, amazed at how light and feeble the older man felt. He half-carried, half-dragged him to a chair and forced him to sit down.

"Can you understand me?" asked Robert, still holding Gold's arms to his sides.

"Behold, thou art fair, my love," intoned Gold in a cracking voice. "Thou hast dove's eyes within thy locks; thy hair is as a flock of goats, that appear from Mount Gilead."

"Thomas!" said Robert harshly, shaking him. "Do you know who I am?"

"Thy lips are like a thread of scarlet," continued Gold, never taking his eyes off the faerie, "and thy speech is comely. Thy temples are like a piece of pomegranate within thy locks."

Robert walked in front of Gold and slapped his face.

"Come out of it!" he snapped. "You've practically brained my friend! I've got to get a doctor in here!"

Gold turned to face the female faerie.

"Thy two breasts are like two young roes that are twins, which feed among the lilies."

"Damn it, Thomas!"

Another slap.

"Thou art all fair, my love. There is no spot in thee."

"Snap out of it! I've got to get you back home before the doctor arrives!"

Gold blinked furiously. "Home?" he mumbled.

"Yes, home! I've sent Simon and Christina ahead, but I've got to get you out of here. Try to get hold of yourself."

"*Simon?*" repeated Gold, sanity briefly returning to his eyes, followed by an expression of terror. He looked wildly around the room. "Where is he?"

"I just told you. He's on his way home."

Gold relaxed, his lean body sagging onto the chair.

Robert stared at him for a moment.

"Will you be all right now? Can I turn my back on you for a minute?"

Gold nodded weakly.

Robert walked to a vidphone, covered the camera so that no one could see the room, and placed an emergency call for a Jesus Pure doctor.

Then he walked over to the two faeries. Gold had ripped the translator off the male, but the female's was working, and he told her, as succinctly and apologetically as he could, that his father-in-law was a desperately sick man, that he was not responsible for his actions, and that someone would be coming by in a moment to take them back to the ship. The Church of the Purity of Jesus Christ, he added, would accept full responsibility for what had happened, and would agree to any reasonable reparations that were demanded.

He returned to Gold.

"Can you walk?" he asked.

"I don't know," mumbled Gold.

"Try."

Gold got shakily to his feet.

"I have to get you out of here before anyone arrives," said Robert. "Do you think you can make it to your dressing room?"

Gold nodded.

"Then let's go."

Robert supported the older man as they walked out into the corridor and back to Gold's room, then helped him to lie down on a couch.

"I'm going to leave you for a few minutes now," said Robert, speaking as if to a small child. "I'll be right down the hallway. Just try to relax."

Gold, his eyes closed, nodded absently, and Robert left the room, locking the door behind him.

He put in a quick call to his staff aboard the ship, then approached the faeries and told them to follow him out into the corridor. He took them to an empty room he had passed earlier, told them to remain there, and reassured them once again that someone would arrive shortly to take them back to the ship.

He then returned to his assistant, who was still groggy but slowly regaining his senses.

"How are you doing?" he asked.

The man muttered something unintelligible.

"Do you know who hit you?"

"Gold or the faeries, one or the other," came the mumbled answer.

"But you're not sure which?"

The man shook his head, then moaned in pain. "No."

"I've sent for a doctor," said Robert. "He'll be here in a couple of minutes. He's going to ask you the same question."

"Maybe I'll remember by then."

"And maybe you won't," said Robert. "I think

you'd be better off telling him just what you told me—that you don't know who hit you. We don't want to cause a political or racial incident if you're not one hundred percent sure."

"All right," said the man, closing his eyes and placing his hands to his head. "Whatever you say."

"I'm going to leave you alone now," said Robert. "But the doctor will be here very soon. Tell him I'll check with him later and pick up the bill. All right?"

"Fine," muttered the man.

Robert then returned to Gold's room. He waited until the corridor was empty, commanded the door to open, and gingerly entered the room, fully prepared to ward off another attack—but Gold was still on the couch, exactly as Robert had left him.

"How are you feeling now?" asked Robert, approaching him. "Any better?"

"The joints of thy thighs are like jewels," intoned Gold, staring aimlessly into space. "Thy naval is like a round goblet, which wanteth not liquor."

Robert looked down at the pale, tortured, emaciated man.

"Come on," he said gently, helping Gold to his feet. "It's time to go home."

"Make haste, my beloved, and be thou like to a roe upon the mountains of spices."

15

"Finally!" exclaimed Simon, getting to his feet as Robert and Gold appeared in the doorway of the apartment. He noticed the scratches on Gold's face. "Are you all right, Father?"

Gold nodded his head.

Christina remained seated, but Corinne approached him solicitously, and he leaned even more heavily on Robert's shoulder.

"I'm fine," he said weakly. "Leave me alone."

"You!" said Simon furiously, pointing at Robert. "If you ever try to hit me again, I'm going to make you sorry you were ever born!"

"Fine," said Robert, obviously unimpressed with the threat. "In the meantime, help me get your father to his bedroom."

"*I'll* help you," said Corinne, wrapping Gold's free arm around her shoulders.

"You've been with him for almost an hour," said Simon, so enraged that he didn't notice that he was blocking their way. "Didn't you ever think of putting some medication on those scratches?"

"They're superficial," answered Robert. "It was more important to get him home."

"Well, now that he's here, he doesn't need *you* anymore!" said Simon, taking Robert's place at his father's side.

"I want to lie down," murmured Gold.

"Of course, Father," said Simon. "Let me help you."

He and Corinne led Gold through the living room to the doorway of the bedroom, where Gold paused and shrugged his shoulders until they both released him.

"Can you make it the rest of the way yourself, Father?" asked Simon.

"I'll help him get out of his clothes and put him to bed," said Corinne.

Gold looked down at his wife with an unmistakable expression of revulsion, then stepped inside the bedroom alone and locked the door behind him. Corinne stood facing the door, her shoulders sagging, while Simon turned back into the living room.

Robert sat down next to Christina and put an arm around her. She remained motionless, her face mirroring her dismay.

"What took you so long?" demanded Simon.

"I had to be very careful bringing him home," replied Robert. "We don't want any publicity over this."

"Well, there's going to be publicity, and plenty of it!" snapped Simon. "I intend to register an official complaint against the Andricans the first thing in the morning."

"I don't think that would be a very wise thing to do, Simon," said Robert.

"Well, I'm just not gifted with your wisdom," said Simon nastily. "For example, I would have thought hitting a man who was trying to save his father wasn't a very wise thing either!"

"Oh, shut up, Simon!" snapped Christina. "He didn't do you any damage, and you know it!"

"Why did he make me leave?" demanded Simon. "I could have helped!"

"I doubt it," said Robert.

Simon stared contemptuously at him. "Maybe I'm not a specialist in street brawling, like some members of this family, but my father was trying to fend off an attack by a crazed alien—and *you* wouldn't even come to his aid until you were alone and could claim all the credit for it!"

"Is that why you think I made you leave?" asked Robert unbelievingly.

"What other possible reason could you have?" demanded Simon.

Robert snorted disgustedly. "You're a fool."

"Mother," said Christina, suddenly noticing Corinne was still standing before the bedroom door. "Please sit down."

Corinne sighed and rejoined them. "He's been behaving so *strangely* these last few weeks," she said.

"That's because he's not a well man," responded Christina. She turned and looked directly at Simon. "He's *sick*, Simon—sicker than you think."

"He'll be fine in a few days," said Simon defensively. "He just needs a little rest."

She shook her head. "He needs more than rest, Simon. He needs help." She paused. "You don't have any idea what I'm talking about, do you?"

"He's very tired," offered Corinne. "Sometimes he behaves oddly when he's been working too hard."

"Please, Mother!" said Simon irritably. "He's more than tired."

"That's what I've been trying to tell you," said Christina.

"I don't know *what* you've been trying to tell me, except that it's all right for Robert to hit me when he feels like it!"

"Forget about Robert, and forget about yourself!" said Christine. "Can't you see what's been happening? He's not well!"

"You keep saying that!" snapped Simon. "All right, he's not well. We'll take him to a doctor and he'll *get* well!"

"I've tried to get him to go to one for the past month," said Corinne. "But he keeps refusing."

"We're not going to *ask* him if he wants to go," said Robert. "We're going to tell him he's *got* to."

"You're not telling my father anything!" said Simon. "And if he doesn't want to go to a doctor, that's his decision. God will give him the strength to continue his work."

"He's not capable of making that decision, Simon," said Robert.

"Who is?" said Simon contemptuously. "You?"

"You utter fool!" cried Christina. "Are you so blind that you still don't understand what I'm trying to tell you?" She turned to Corinne. "You lived day and night with him for thirty-six years. Can't *you* tell that something's terribly wrong?"

"He's been snappish, and he's had trouble sleeping," she said, "but he's been like that before. You were too young to remember, but once, about twenty-five years ago, he had a bleeding ulcer and didn't tell anyone until—"

"I'm not talking about a bleeding ulcer!" screamed Christina in frustration. "My God, can't either of you see it?"

"See *what*?" said Simon peevishly. "All I see is a man who stopped me from helping my father ward off a violent attack by an alien."

Christina turned to Robert. "Will you tell him, for God's sake, or do *I* have to?"

"Simon," said Robert, trying to submerge the antagonism he felt toward his brother-in-law, "I didn't save your father from the Andrican."

"What are you talking about? Of course you did!"

Robert shook his head. "I had to save the Andrican from your father."

"That's a lie!" exploded Simon.

"No, Simon. It's the truth."

"Why would Father attack an Andrican?"

Robert looked briefly at Christina, then turned back to Simon. "Because his body isn't the only part of him that's sick."

Simon was on his feet instantly, his hands balled into fists. "You take that back! Thomas Gold is as sane as you are!"

"Taking it back won't change the truth of it," said Robert. "Look at his behavior pattern over the last few weeks. He can't sleep, he's moody, half the time he can't even put a coherent sentence together."

"He's been edgy, that's all. He's been working on his sermon."

"You heard him tonight, Simon," said Robert. "He didn't put two seconds of work into that sermon."

"He *did*! He spent all week working on it!"

"Was that the kind of sermon he usually produces after he's worked so long and so hard?" asked Robert.

"I'll prove it to you!" shouted Simon. "I'll bring it up on his computer!"

"I don't think that's a very good idea," said Robert.

"You just don't want to admit you're wrong, and that you've defamed a great man," said Simon.

"He's ordered us all to leave his computer alone, Simon," said Christina, a note of desperation in her voice. "I think we should honor his wishes."

"He won't mind," said Simon confidently. "Not if it's used to clear his good name."

"I don't think you should do this, Simon," said Corinne.

"So you're siding with *them*?"

"I'm siding with your father," she replied. "Unlike you and your sister, I don't worship him. I just love him, and I don't *want* to know what's in the computer."

"He'd be touched by your faith in him," said Simon sardonically. He walked to the office doorway. "I'll be out in a minute or two, and then I expect an apology from each of you. Not to *me*," he added, "but to *him*."

He entered the office and the door slid shut behind him.

There was a momentary silence.

"How did it happen?" asked Christina numbly. "How *could* it happen to a man like that?"

"You speak about him as if he were a saint," said Corinne gently. "And he's not. He's just a man."

"Mother, you don't even know what I'm talking about!"

"You're talking about your father," replied Corinne. "That's all that's important."

Christina turned her tortured gaze on her husband. "He was up there for only five hours. *Five hours!* Maybe Fiona Bradley's on the right side after all! Maybe it's finally Satan's turn to win!"

Robert put an arm around her, and she buried her face on his shoulder, her body finally convulsed by the sobs that she had been holding back.

"We're going to have to hunt up a doctor who can keep his mouth shut," said Robert at last. "And I think he'll have to be treated right here in the apartment. I don't think either he or the church can stand the publicity he'll receive if we move him to a clinic." He paused. "Right now anyone who saw the sermon probably thinks he was just having an off night—and most of them will forget what they saw soon enough. What we've got to do now is control the damage and keep it from spreading."

"You talk about it as if it were some kind of public relations campaign, instead of a man's soul!" said Christina bitterly.

"He'll live," responded Robert. "But we can't let one man's problems destroy the church or the cause he's fought for. The fact that Thomas Gold had a human weakness must not be the downfall of everything he's worked for."

"I know," said Christina. "It just seems so . . . so dispassionate to be discussing it like this."

Robert sighed. "I'm sorry. But we have to decide upon a course of action. And maybe, because of my work, I've been a little less sheltered than you and Simon. Believe me, I've seen Men and aliens both commit far greater sins than your father will ever commit."

"I don't care about Men and aliens. I just care about my father."

"I know," agreed Robert. "He's a fine and decent man who's spent every day of his life staring temptation in the eye and turning away from it. He just faced one temptation too many. Under other circumstances, he might have reacted in a totally different manner."

"That's very small comfort, to me *or* to him," said Christina bitterly.

"I'm a scientist," answered Robert apologetically. "I'm better at analyzing problems than finding comforting things to say about them. I feel for your father, I ache and bleed for him just as you do—but I also see that some important decisions have to be made."

Suddenly Simon reentered the room, his face drawn and pale. He walked, trancelike, to a chair and sat down heavily.

There was a long, tense silence.

"I can't believe it!" he muttered at last.

"I'm sorry, Simon" said Robert sympathetically.

"My own father!" said Simon, his face tortured. "How *could* he?"

"Whatever it is, he couldn't help himself, Simon," said Corinne.

"You!" he said, turning upon her. "You *knew* something was wrong all along! You *had* to know!"

"Even if I did, what could I have done about it?"

"You could have told me. I might have saved him!"

"Saved him?" asked Robert, puzzled.

"From hell," said Simon bitterly. "His actions have condemned him to everlasting perdition."

"Nonsense," said Robert. "He's not responsible for his actions, Simon. He's mentally incompetent."

"We are *all* responsible for our actions!" said Simon in agonized tones. "I begged him not to go up to that place. I *begged* him!"

"Don't blame yourself, Simon," said Corinne. "If anyone's responsible for what's happened to him, it's me."

"You?" said Simon distractedly.

"I should have been a better wife to him. I should have done more. Obviously I didn't satisfy all his needs."

"You foolish, empty-headed woman!" snapped Simon. "Do you realize what you're saying?"

"Don't speak to me like that!"

He pointed a trembling finger at her. "Don't you *ever* say that my father *needed* what those creatures offered!"

"Creatures?" asked Corinne. "What creatures?"

"They're not *creatures*, Simon," said Christina. "They're sentient beings, and you tried to use them for your own purposes, just as the *Velvet Comet* uses them for *its* purposes."

"You mean the Andricans?" asked Corinne curiously.

"What do you think we've been talking about?" said Christina.

"They're malevolent, evil *things*, and they corrupted the most noble man I've ever known!" raged Simon. "And I'm going to make them pay dearly for it, as God is my witness!"

"Get a grip on yourself, Simon," interjected Robert. "We've got some decisions to make. Your father needs psychiatric treatment."

"It doesn't matter," said Simon dully.

"What are you talking about?" demanded Robert. "He's sick. He needs professional help."

"Don't you understand?" grated Simon in tortured tones. "He's going to spend all eternity in hell, and here you are talking about how to treat him for the most insignificant speck of time. His *soul* is lost, and you're worrying about his *mind*!"

"Don't talk rubbish!" snapped Robert. "God isn't going to punish him for being ill."

"What do *you* know about it? You call yourself a Jesus Pure, but you eat meat, and you sing, and you see sin and you make no attempt to fight it. You turned your back on your religion to pursue the petty, meaningless truths of agnostic science—so don't you tell me what God will or won't do!"

"Simon, you've had a terrible shock," said Robert, "but so have all the rest of us. Instead of recriminations, it seems to me that we ought to be thinking about what's best for your father."

"He's lost already," said Simon. "We've got to stop this from ever happening to anyone else."

"Damn it!" exploded Robert. "He's not lost! He's lying on a bed in the next room, and he needs our help!"

"Fool!" snapped Simon. "The church fights an unending battle against the forces of evil, and my father has become a casualty. Don't you understand? He was tempted, and he succumbed! His soul has been made unspeakably unclean; no doctor can put it right again!"

"I hope that if I ever fall from the path of righteousness," said Robert, "I receive more compassion from those I love than you're showing *him*."

Simon's face twisted in agony.

"Do you think I don't love him, or that I don't share his pain?" he said, his voice breaking. "He's my *father*! If I could take his pain and his sin as my own, I would. If I could accept his eternal punishment as my own, I'd bear it gladly. But I can't! He can't be redeemed. He can only be avenged!"

Suddenly he froze, his gaze fixed on a point across the room, and they all turned to see Thomas Gold supporting himself against the framework of the bedroom doorway.

"I heard voices shouting," said Gold tiredly. "Is everyone all right?"

Christina quickly went to him.

"Everything's fine, Father," she said gently. "Let me help you back to bed."

He shook his head. "I have to talk to Simon."

Simon stared at him, his expression a mixture of pity and repugnance.

"I can't!" he whispered.

Gold reached his hand out, as if he could touch his son across the intervening twenty feet.

"Simon," he said.

Simon shook his head. "I have to go."

"Please . . ." mumbled Gold.

Simon backed away until he reached the front door, then ordered it open.

"I loved you, Father!" he said, tears streaming down his face. "I truly did!"

Then he was gone, and the door slid shut behind him.

"I wanted to talk to him," Gold said to Christina. "I wanted to . . ." His voice trailed off.

"He's upset, Father," she said soothingly. "He'll be back."

"Will he?"

"Of course he will," replied Christina. "You heard him. He loves you. Let me take you back to bed now."

"It's not necessary," he said. "I'm feeling stronger."

"Would you like to sit with us, then?" asked Corinne.

He gave her a look of complete indifference, and shook his head. "I'll rest later. I have work to do." He turned supplicatingly to Christina. "Please help me over to my office."

"Your office?" she repeated, frowning.

He nodded weakly.

"I have to go back to work."

"No you don't, Father. You're going to take a vacation now. You've been working too hard."

"My computer," he mumbled. "I need my computer."

"Why don't you come in here and join us?" said Robert.

Gold stared wildly at him.

"I want my computer," he said, his voice gathering strength, his expression suddenly that of a cornered animal. "You can't keep me from it!"

"Please, Father ... " said Christina, tugging gently at his arm.

He pushed her away and shambled to his office door.

"Keep away from me! I have work to do!"

"Don't go in there, Thomas," said Robert, getting to his feet. "Come sit with us instead."

"You can't keep me from my work!"

"It can wait until tomorrow," said Robert, taking a tentative step toward him.

"I'm locking the door!" said Gold. "And God help anyone who tries to break it down!"

He darted into the office, and the door slid into place and locked before Robert could reach him.

And while his family tried to decide what action to take, Thomas Gold walked to his computer and stroked it lovingly with a frail, shaking hand.

"They thought they could keep me away from you," he whispered, his eyes alight with excitement. "They thought they could lock me away, that they could make me forget about you. That's what they thought." He chuckled. "They thought so, they thought so, but they were wrong. Activate."

The computer hummed to life.

"Hello," said Gold a moment later, when the holograph of an unclad faerie hovered above the computer. His hand reached out and caressed the empty space that was occupied by the image.

"I've missed you," he said tenderly.

16

Attila was sitting in his office, sipping a cup of coffee and going over the evening duty roster, when the Steel Butterfly's holograph suddenly appeared over his computer.

"What's up?" he asked.

"I've just checked over the next shuttle's list of incoming passengers, and I think we're about to get a rather important visitor," she informed him.

"Oh?"

"He gave a phony name, and his ID checks out—but it's Thomas Gold just the same."

Attila frowned. "You're sure? I mean, after that broadcast the other night, I'd think this is the *last* place his people would let him come."

"His people probably don't know anything about it," replied the Steel Butterfly. "A man like Gold wouldn't have too much trouble finding a way to sneak out of wherever they're keeping him. He may be crazy, but he isn't stupid."

"If his ID checks out, what makes you so sure it's Gold?" persisted Attila.

"Cupid, you tell him."

"He has tried to disguise himself, but there is no question that he is Doctor Thomas Gold," said the computer. "Height, six feet four inches. Weight, 142 pounds. Mild irregularity in heartbeat. There is a small mole on the left corner of his upper lip. His hair texture is—"

"All right, I'm convinced," interrupted Attila. "Where did you get all this? From the shuttle's computer?"

"Yes, Attila," answered Cupid.

"And you've compared it to your own file on Thomas Gold?"

"That's correct."

Attila shrugged. "I was wrong. But I sure as hell never thought I'd see him again." He looked up at the Steel Butterfly's image. "We'll detain him at the airlock, of course," he said. "But then what? Do you want to contact someone to come and get him, or do you think we should get a little publicity out of it?"

"Oh, no," she said with a smile. "*You're* the Chief of Security, and this is a Security problem. I'm happy to warn you that he's on his way, but I wouldn't presume to tell you what to do about it."

"Thanks," he said sardonically. "Which shuttle is he on?"

"Delta."

"Delta," he repeated. "That's due to dock in, let me see . . . " He checked his timepiece. "Seven minutes." He got to his feet. "I'd better get moving. Thanks for all the advance notice you gave me," he added with a touch of irony.

He broke the communication, had his computer check to see if the tramcar was at his end of the Mall, discovered that it wasn't, and elected to ride the slidewalk to the airlock rather than wait for the car.

He arrived at the airlock just as Shuttle Delta was beginning its docking maneuvers.

"Cupid?"

"Yes, Attila?"

"What name is Gold using?"

"James Westerman, Jr."

"Patch me through to Delta."

The pilot's face appeared above the nearest computer terminal.

"Hello, Attila," she said. "What can I do for you?"

"You've got a passenger traveling under the name of James Westerman, Jr."

She checked her passenger list. "Right."

"Have one of the attendants find some way to delay him—subtly, if possible—until everyone else is off the shuttle. Then let him off."

"Is he dangerous?" she asked.

"Only to himself."

"You're not giving us much time to set this up," said the pilot. "I think I'd better mess up the docking procedure and take another run at it. Otherwise, by the time I manage to speak to attendants in private and inform them of the situation, he might already be disembarking."

"I'll make it easy for you," said Attila. "Put my voice on your public-address system."

She reached forward and touched something out of the range of the camera, then nodded.

"Attention, Shuttle Delta," he announced. "Dock H is committed to Shuttle Epsilon. Please enter a holding pattern until we can confirm a dock for you." He paused long enough to light up a small, thin Alphard cigar and count silently to one hundred. "Shuttle Delta, you have been cleared for Dock C."

It took the shuttle about eight minutes to dock, during which time Attila determined that there were seventeen passengers aboard it. A moment later they began entering the airlock, and he passed them through as quickly as possible.

Finally, when sixteen patrons had cleared the airlock and entered the Mall, he excused all but one burly guard from airlock duty and signaled the pilot to release Gold.

"I'm terribly sorry, sir," said an attendant who entered the airlock with the minister. "Our scanner must be malfunctioning. But I assure you that it *did* register a hand weapon."

"It's all right," muttered Gold.

"If you wish to file an official complaint, my name is—"

"It's all right, I said!" snapped Gold.

He turned away from the attendant and faced Attila, who couldn't believe his eyes.

Gold's formerly pale cheeks and forehead were covered with unevenly applied makeup, and his hairline was almost two inches higher, with day-old stubble showing where he had shaved it. He had dyed his sideburns black, but the job was a sloppy one, and some of the color had smeared onto his right ear. It would have been laughable, decided the Security chief, were it not so pathetic.

"We meet again, Doctor Gold," said Attila, unable to keep from staring at the minister's face.

"There must be some mistake," said Gold. "My name is James Westerman."

"You're Thomas Gold."

Gold pulled out an identification card. "You are

in error, as you can plainly see. I am James Westerman, Jr., and you are detaining me illegally."

"Do any members of your church know you're up here?" asked Attila.

"I have no church!" snapped Gold. "I am a businessman from the Zeta Piscium system, and you are an insolent hireling! Now let me pass!"

Attila shook his head. "Not a chance, Doctor Gold. But if you'll reenter Shuttle Delta and wait for it to depart, I won't let anyone know you were up here."

"*No!*" bellowed Gold. "I am a patron! You can't keep me off the *Comet!*"

"I'm the Chief of Security," said Attila calmly. "I can refuse entrance to anyone who in my opinion will be a disruptive influence."

Gold seemed disoriented for a moment, then dug a hand into his pocket and withdrew a huge sheaf of thousand-credit notes. "But I can pay!" he said, his voice suddenly desperate and whining. "I have money! Isn't that all you care about?" He waved the notes in Attila's face. "Don't you understand? I can pay!"

"Where did you get all that money?" asked Attila.

Gold's eyes narrowed. "I told you—I'm a businessman."

"You're a minister, and you've lived in poverty for years," said Attila. "What did you do—rob your church?"

"Take it!" pleaded Gold, pushing the wad of notes up against Attila's chest and releasing it. Tears came to his eyes. "Take it! Keep some of it for yourself, I don't care—but for God's sake, let me pass!"

"Guard," said Attila, nodding to the burly green-clad man who had been watching Gold with horrified fascination. "Doctor Gold is going to be leaving us now. Please escort him back onto Shuttle Delta."

"No!" screamed Gold. "I've got to . . . just once . . . before . . . I beg of you!"

"Come along, sir," said the guard, taking Gold by the arm.

Gold pulled loose and raced up to Attila, his long, emaciated fingers clutching at the Security chief's tunic.

"I'll give you whatever you want!" he hissed, his eyes bright and wild. "You want more money? I'll get it! Whatever you want—but you can't keep me away from them!"

"Please come with me, sir," said the guard, walking over and taking a firmer grip on him.

"You can't do this to me!" raged Gold. "I'm a businessman from—from . . . " His voice trailed off as he tried to remember which world he was supposed to have come from.

The guard tried to pull him away, and Gold threw himself to the ground and began screaming incoherently.

"Attila?" said the guard, looking questioningly at the Security chief.

"We can't send him back like this," said Attila as he watched Gold writhing and moaning on the floor, begging for entrance to the *Comet.* He sighed. "Let's get him to the hospital and inform his church of his whereabouts."

Attila lifted Gold to his feet, and he and the guard half-dragged, half-carried him into the bright interior of the *Velvet Comet,* where the Security chief ordered a nearby subordinate to restaff the airlock.

Gold stopped struggling when they were halfway across the Mall. Suddenly his eyes became clear and his demeanor calm.

"Can you walk now, Doctor Gold?" asked Attila, tentatively loosening his grip on Gold's shoulder.

Gold nodded, then looked at his surroundings.

"This is wrong," he announced, puzzled.

"What is, Doctor Gold?"

"Everything," he said. "It always starts with the imp, and then the black unicorn."

"Perhaps they're waitng for you in the hospital," suggested Attila.

Gold considered the statement, then nodded his head tentatively.

"Perhaps," he agreed. His face lit up with delight. "And if *they* are, then so are the faeries!"

"I wouldn't be a bit surprised," said Attila soothingly.

"Then let's hurry!" said Gold. "I can't keep them waiting any longer!"

"Why don't you run ahead and make sure they're waiting?" said Attila to the guard.

The man nodded and raced off to alert the medical staff, while Thomas Gold, his face glowing with childlike enthusiasm, his words a torrent of innocent dreams and sinister fantasies, followed Attila.

17

The Steel Butterfly frowned at Attila's image.

"*Another* one?" she repeated.

The Security chief nodded. "With a very ingenious plastic weapon. The scanner didn't recognize it at first." He paused. "She came closer to getting through than any of the others. We haven't put her under hypnosis yet, but I think it's safe to assume that you were her primary target."

"Me? Why not you?"

"Because if she was here to kill me, she could have done it right there in the airlock."

"I *told* you we weren't going to be happy with whoever replaced Thomas Gold," said the Steel Butterfly, sipping her drink. "How many does that make now?"

"Four this week, and seven in the two months since they locked Gold away," replied Attila.

"What's the matter with them anyway?" she demanded. "I thought Jesus Pures were supposed to be against violence!"

"My own opinion is that the son is crazier than the father," answered the Security chief. "Did you hear him last night?"

She shook her head. "Why bother? It's the same drivel he's been spouting for the past six weeks."

"Not quite," said Attila. "It's actually getting more vehement. Cupid?"

"Yes, Attila?" said the computer.

"Play the last couple of minutes of Simon Gold's most recent broadcast for the Steel Butterfly."

Instantly Attila's holograph vanished, to be replaced by the fierce, unsmiling visage of Simon Gold.

"If thy hand offend thee, cut it off!" he intoned, staring righteously into the camera. "What does this mean? Simply that there are certain objects that are beyond salvation. They are past all hope of redemption, and must be forcibly removed from the affairs of Men. The *Velvet Comet* is such an object."

He looked out at his audience.

"It destroyed my father," he said fiercely. "And if it can destroy Thomas Gold, it can destroy anyone!"

He paused for that thought to sink in.

"The *Velvet Comet* is a blight upon the galaxy, and an offense to all moral men and women. What does the Bible tell us to do?"

He smiled with grim satisfaction as hundreds of voices from his audience told him exactly what action to take.

"He who loves his God the best will be he who puts an end to that wicked, sinful ship!"

The roar of approval from the audience was deafening—and then the holograph blinked out of existence, to be replaced by Attila's image.

"Some prayer meeting, eh?" he said grimly.

"Can't we have him arrested?" asked the Steel Butterfly. "He's actually exhorting them to come up here and kill us!"

Attila shook his head. "I already spoke to Vainmill's legal department. All he actually said was that he wanted to see the *Comet* put out of business. The implication was clear—but it's still just an implication. I mean, hell, there are probably a hundred *other* ways to shut us down. He can always claim that he was referring to one of them."

"Can't we slap an injunction on him anyway—something to keep him off the air?"

"Probably—but Vainmill won't do it."

"Why not?"

"For the same reason they wouldn't do it to his father. They don't want to make a martyr out of him."

"But Thomas Gold only threatened economic boycotts; his son is threatening us with violence."

Attila grimaced. "Why don't you ask Fiona Bradley which she prefers—violence against *us*, or an economic boycott directed against Vainmill?"

"Maybe you and I can arrange a private meeting with Simon Gold," she suggested.

"I doubt it—and he's not Simon Gold anymore. As of yesterday, his name, title, call it what you will, is Simon the Eradicator."

"Why is he carrying on like this?" she asked in frustration. "It's not *our* fault that his father became obsessed with the faeries and went crazy!"

"He's got to blame *some*one," said Attila. "And along with having to lock Gold away, I gather his mother had a series of strokes about a month ago. She's been in an intensive-care unit ever since."

"Maybe someone ought to tell him that killing us and closing down the *Comet* isn't going to solve either of those problems," said the Steel Butterfly.

"*I'd* settle for his remembering that he's supposed to be against violence," replied Attila. "That woman today came *very* close to passing through the airlock."

"Well, what do you propose to do about these fanatics?" demanded the Steel Butterfly. "Pretty soon one of them *will* get through."

"I've been giving it some serious thought," admitted Attila.

"And?"

"And I think we should put a ban on daytrippers—at least until Simon calms down."

"What will banning the daytrippers accomplish?"

"Most of them are just shoppers," answered Attila. "They spend all their time in the Mall and never enter the brothel." He paused. "Our security is much better within the brothel than outside it. We've got cameras positioned in every room and scanners all the hell over the place. But the Mall is a different matter: it's almost two miles long, and it's got five hundred and sixty-two stores and boutiques in it."

"I know all this," she said impatiently. "Get to the point."

"The point is simply this: no one is going to smuggle a weapon into the brothel, not even a pocket knife. But after today's experience, I'm not convinced that they can't smuggle *parts* of a weapon, especially a plastic one, into the Mall. They can hide the parts in secret locations inside stores, and eventually someone who knows how to assemble and use it will come up here and do just that. He won't have to enter the brothel; he can just stand in the Mall and start blowing away the patrons. The effect will be the same: we can't stay in business if we can't protect our clientele."

"Have you spoken to Constantine about this?" asked the Steel Butterfly.

"I thought I'd better talk to you first," said Attila. "For one thing, I don't think the shops are going to be very happy about it, and if I don't have your complete support Constantine will never buy it."

"True," she said, lowering her head in thought. Finally she looked up at his image. "How long would you enforce the ban?"

"That depends upon our friend Simon the Eradicator. I'd certainly keep it in force as long as he keeps telling his people that God will love them even more if they destroy us."

"What if he keeps it up for a year?" she asked.

"Then we won't allow daytrippers for a year," he replied. He paused. "Look, if some divinely inspired Jesus Pure comes up here and wipes out three hundred patrons in the Mall, we're not going to have to worry about the shopkeepers anyway. We'll be out of business ten minutes later."

She sighed. "All right. Let's get hold of Constantine and see if we can persuade him to sanction it."

She placed three calls before she even got through to his personal secretary, and she was then informed that he would contact her an hour later, when he got out of a meeting with Fiona Bradley.

The call came through exactly as scheduled, and Attila was immediately patched into it.

"This had better be important," said Constantine, obviously annoyed at having his schedule disrupted. "I'm due at another meeting in five minutes."

"I think it is," said the Steel Butterfly. "Have you heard Simon Gold lately?"

Constantine smiled. "Simon the Eradicator? Don't worry about him. He's just out for publicity."

"He damned near got it," she said. "We caught an armed Jesus Pure trying to get onto the *Comet* today. It was the seventh in two months."

"There are madmen in every religion. I think Tom Gold proved that."

"I don't think you realize the gravity of the situation," interjected Attila.

Constantine checked his timepiece, and frowned. "All right. You tell me—and try to be brief."

The Security chief explained how the plastic weapon had escaped Cupid's preliminary inspection, outlined the methodology for smuggling a disassembled weapon into one of the Mall's stores, and offered his solution.

"Out of the question," said Constantine when Attila had finished. "The shops would consider it a breach of contract, and they'd be right. Ninety percent of them would move out within a month."

"How many of them will move out if a gunman actually gets into the Mall?" replied Attila.

"It's *your* job to see to it that such an eventuality doesn't come to pass."

"Won't you at least consider it?" asked the Steel Butterfly.

"Don't be ridiculous," answered Constantine. "The *Velvet Comet* exists to make money. Once it stops turning a profit, we won't need Simon Gold's urging to shut it down."

"It will make a profit with or without the stores," she persisted. "And this is only a temporary measure—just until he stops encouraging his followers to attack us."

"And what if he never stops?" demanded Constantine. "Or let's put the best possible face on it: what if he drops dead next month and the Jesus Pure disband? How am I going to convince any merchant to rent a store in the Mall if he knows that I'll shut him down at the first sign of trouble?" He paused. "Look—I appreciate your concern, but the two of you are taking an extremely narow view of the situation. The stores stay open."

"That's your final word?" asked Attila.

"It is."

"Will you at least discuss it with Fiona Bradley?" asked the Steel Butterfly.

"If Fiona Bradley wanted to deal with the day-in, day-out problems of the Entertainment and Leisure Divison, she wouldn't have put me in charge of it," said Constantine, his tone increasingly irritated. "Now if you'll excuse me, I have a meeting to attend."

He broke the connection.

"Well, we tried," said the Steel Butterfly.

"Should we make an attempt to get through to Fiona Bradley ourselves?" asked Attila.

She shook her head. "We'd be usurping Constantine's authority. I think he'd fire us just for that." She sighed. "I guess we'll just have to hope that Cupid will be able to keep spotting potential mass murderers."

"Or that Simon Gold will tone down his attacks," added Attila. "Who would have thought he would publicly admit that Gold went crazy over the faeries? It takes away the one weapon I was sure we'd be able to use against Gold's successor."

"You mean the disk of the scene in my office?"

He nodded. "It's totally worthless now."

"Except as a weapon against *us*," she said ironically. "If anyone should ever come across it, Constantine will realize that we lied to him."

"It's pretty well hidden," he assured her. "We'll both be retired before anyone finds it."

"Cupid!" she said sharply.

"Yes, madam?" said the computer.

"Put this conversation in my Priority file, retroactive to the moment when Richard Constantine broke contact with us."

"Done," announced the computer instantly.

She looked at Attila. "We'd better not mention that disk again. All anyone has to do is hear us speak about it and they'll know it exists—and once they know what they're looking for, they'll find it."

"I agree." A light flashed on his desk. "Another problem at the airlock," he announced. "What is it, Cupid?"

"I have scanned patron Marianna Vittore of Pollux IV and discovered a subclinical venereal disease. She is being discreetly escorted to the hospital for treatment, and should be able to proceed to the brothel in approximately twenty minutes."

Attila relaxed. "Thank God for small favors. Every time I see that damned light, I think another Jesus Pure is trying to sneak in."

"Well, I guess all we can do is keep spotting them and sending them back," sighed the Steel Butterfly. "Who knows? Maybe they'll get tired of it before we do."

"Somehow I don't think that's too likely," replied Attila.

"Neither do I," she agreed. "Well, I suppose we'd better get back to work."

"I guess so," he said wearily, reaching out to break the connection.

And, as the Steel Butterfly and Attila went about their business aboard the *Velvet Comet*, four thousand miles beneath them Simon the Eradicator put his Bible down and began plotting the final step in his campaign to make certain that the orbiting brothel which had destroyed his father was permanently decommissioned.

18

"Red Alert!"

Attila sat up in his bed.

"What the hell are you talking about?"

"Red Alert, Attila," repeated Cupid.

"Come on!" he said irritably. "There hasn't been a Red Alert since the *Comet* was activated."

"That is true, Attila. Nonetheless, there is currently a condition of Red Alert."

Attila rubbed his eyes and ran a hand through his hair.

"All right," he said, starting to get dressed. "What's the situation?"

"Simon the Eradicator, whom I believe you know as Simon Gold, has docked his ship at the *Velvet Comet* and threatens to destroy the *Comet*—and himself with it—if his demands are not met."

"Can you get me a visual?" asked Attila, suddenly wide awake.

"Certainly," replied Cupid, creating a hologram of a private ship at Dock H.

"That's him?"

"Yes, Attila."

"Does he actually have any explosives aboard his ship?"

"If he didn't, I would not have signaled a Red Alert."

"What kind and how powerful?" demanded Attila, stepping into his pants.

"He has a single thermonuclear fission device. The detonator has been activated, and my scanners tell me that it is connected to his ship's control panel, enabling him to explode it whenever he wishes."

"Can you deactivate it?"

"Not without Simon the Eradicator's consent," answered Cupid.

Attila studied the holograph more closely.

"Give me the worst-possible scenario," he ordered.

"He detonates the bomb and the *Velvet Comet* is literally ripped apart."

"Now give me a best-possible scenario that includes detonation."

"He detonates the bomb, the *Velvet Comet* suffers minimal structural damage, and the radiation within the *Comet* falls to a minimally acceptable level in thirteen years."

Attila muttered a curse.

"All right—so we can't have him detonating his bomb under any circumstances. What are his demands?"

"That the *Velvet Comet* be permanently shut down."

"What kind of time frame are we talking about?" asked Attila.

"He has given Vainmill eight hours to accede to his demands, which were made seven minutes ago."

"Has he got a communications channel to Richard Constantine or Fiona Bradley?"

"He does not."

"Then he wants us to deliver the message?"

"He has not said so, but it seems the logical conclusion."

"Does the Steel Butterfly know what's going on?"

"When I declare a condition of Red Alert, I am compelled to inform all crew members and patrons."

"You mean the patrons know too?" demanded Attila.

"I think it is a bad idea," commented Cupid. "It is very likely to cause a panic among them. But I am unable to bypass that portion of my programming."

"Wonderful," muttered Attila. He paused in thought for a moment. "Patch me through to Cordero."

The image of a man in a green uniform appeared.

"Have we got ourselves a full-scale panic yet?" asked Attila.

The Security man shook his head. "They're nervous and they're scared, but the situation's not out of control yet."

"It'll get worse," said Attila. "I'm putting you in charge of them. I'm going to stay here and see what I can do about Simon Gold."

"Right."

"How many ships and shuttlecraft are docked here?"

"Nineteen shuttles, forty-six private craft, two small cruise ships, and a food cargo ship."

"Enough to evacuate all the patrons and staff if we have to?"

"More than enough, counting the cargo ship."

"Then keep him here. Cupid, get me the Steel Butterfly." Instantly her holograph appeared over his computer terminal. "Who gets to tell Constantine and Bradley?" he asked. "You or me?"

"I've put an emergency call through to Constantine," she said. "That means that I might actually receive a reply within an hour or two."

"Has anyone spoken directly to Simon Gold yet?"

She shook her head. "Not to my knowledge. Cupid tells me that *he* received the message, checked its accuracy with his scanners, and immediately declared a Red Alert."

"Well, I suppose *some*body had better talk to him before he starts getting nervous." He sighed. "I always knew there was a good reason not to be Chief of Security."

"Good luck," she said.

"I have a feeling I'll need it."

He broke the connection, then instructed Cupid to connect him to Simon Gold. A moment later Simon's face and torso blinked into existence.

"You're Simon the Eradicator?" said Attila.

"And you must be the one called Attila," said Simon, staring unblinkingly into his eyes.

"You don't look much like your father," remarked the Security chief.

"I looked a lot more like him before his association with the *Velvet Comet*," answered Simon coldly.

"By the way, do you mind if I see the nuclear device for myself?" asked Attila.

"Not at all," replied Simon, directing his ship's computer to send an image of it to the *Comet*.

"Impressive," said Attila.

"Are you satisfied that I'm in earnest?"

"I don't know. Are you?"

Simon nodded. "In *deadly* earnest."

"And if we don't agree to your terms?"

"Then I am quite prepared to die to ensure that the *Velvet Comet* never again corrupts a single soul." He stared at the camera. "I assure you that I'm not bluffing."

"No," admitted Attila. "I don't think you are."

"Then we have nothing further to say to each other, have we?" said Simon. "I presume that the decison will be made at a higher level."

"I presume so," agreed Attila. "In the meantime, may I make a request?"

"What is it?" asked Simon.

"Your argument is with Vainmill and with the crew of the *Comet*. Will you at least allow our patrons to leave?"

"Ask me again in two hours."

"Will you let them leave then?" persisted Attila.

"We'll see," responded Simon with a grim smile. "In the meantime, I shall allow them this time to reflect upon their sins."

Attila broke the connection, then raised the Steel Butterfly on the intercom.

"Well?" she said.

"He means business," he replied. "Any word from Constantine yet?"

She shook her head. "The staff is doing a good job of keeping the patrons calm, but it can't last forever."

"I've checked the docks, and there are enough ships there to evacuate everyone—*if* we can do it before Simon Gold pushes the button."

"Is Simon Gold really prepared to blow himself up to destroy the *Comet*?" she asked.

"I don't think the thought of death frightens him in the least. He's sure he's going straight to heaven."

"Thomas Gold was always opposed to violence, and yet his son is planning to destroy hundreds of people," she said unbelievingly. "This is madness!"

"Is there any possibility that we can get Thomas Gold to talk his son out of this?" suggested Attila.

The Steel Butterfly sighed deeply. "I already thought of that."

"And?"

"He hasn't said a word since they put him away, except to quote the Song of Solomon—which I gather he does endlessly," she replied. "The man's a raving lunatic. He can't talk anyone into or out of anything." Suddenly she tensed. "Just a minute. I think Constantine is trying to get through to me. Keep monitoring my office."

A moment later Richard Constantine's image appeared.

"This is getting to be a habit," he said severely. "You'd better have a damned good reason for interrupting me."

"Of course I do."

"What is it?"

"You remember we were discussing Simon Gold the other day? Well, his ship is currently docked at the *Comet*. It's armed with a thermonuclear device, and he says that he'll detonate it if Vainmill doesn't agree to decommission the *Comet* within the next seven hours."

The color left Constantine's face.

"Do the patrons know he's there?"

"Cupid told them," put in Attila.

"Our own computer told them?" he repeated unbelievingly.

"It's programmed to inform everyone on the ship of a Red Alert."

"That's great!" snapped Constantine. "Just great!" He paused. "Did Simon Gold say whether he wants the ship closed down in seven hours, or whether he simply wants a decision in seven hours? Maybe we can buy a little time here."

"He wants the ship closed down," replied Attila.

"Damn!" muttered Constantine. "How much do you think he wants?"

"You're dealing with a religious fanatic who thinks he's avenging his father," said the Steel Butterfly. "All he wants is to decommission the ship. Money doesn't mean a thing to him. He thinks God has sent him on a holy mission of destruction."

"Let me talk to him," said Constantine, and Cupid immediately patched him through to Simon's ship.

"Simon Gold, this is Richard Constantine," he announced.

"I know who you are," answered Simon.

"Why are you threatening the lives of the *Comet*'s crew and patrons?"

"Because the *Velvet Comet* is a blight upon humanity, and must be eradicated."

"Even if it means killing hundreds of innocent people?"

Simon stared coldly at Constantine's image. "If they are aboard the *Velvet Comet*, they are not innocent people."

"That's an awful lot of blood to have on your hands."

"I have large hands," replied Simon gravely.

"May I ask you a question?" continued Constantine.

"Go ahead."

"What will you do if we give in to your demands?"

"I don't think I understand you."

"You've got a thermonuclear device, and you'll have seen that this kind of terrorist blackmail can be highly effective against people who cherish human life more than principle," said Constantine. "So my question is: what Vainmill property will you threaten to destroy next?"

"I'd suggest that you worry about *this* one," replied Simon.

"This one's already lost," said Constantine calmly. "Either we'll close it down or you'll blow it up. Either way there will be no *Velvet Comet* tomorrow. What I want to know is why I should yield to your demands. After all, if I don't, at least you and your device won't be a problem tomorrow—but if I give in, what assurance do I have that this conversation won't be repeated at a new Vainmill target every week?"

"You have my word," said Simon.

"What is your word worth?" continued Constantine.

"You'll have to decide for yourself."

"Well, in the meantime, let me tell you what *my* word is worth," said Constantine. "If you will give up your demands right now, I am sure we can work out some method of recompensing you for your time. Do you understand what I'm saying?"

"Of course," replied Simon. "You're saying that you think I'm for sale."

"I think we could further agree not to press criminal charges against you, in exchange for your promise never to use terrorist methods against Vainmill again."

"I have no fear of prison."

"We would also promise to destroy all holographic records of your unfortunate father's rather embarrassing trips to the *Comet*."

"My father is in no condition to care what you do with those records."

"*He* may not be, but we control a number of news media that would love to get their hands on those disks." He paused. "Releasing them certainly couldn't do your church's reputation any good."

"The mere fact that you can make such a threat convinces me that I have chosen the only viable course of action," said Simon.

"There's nothing viable about it. Let's search for some other way to resolve our differences."

"Mr. Constantine, you have seven hours and thirteen minutes left," said Simon, reaching out and breaking connection.

Constantine looked at the images of Attila and the Steel Butterfly.

"Opinions?" he said.

"He's fully prepared to die," said Attila. "Eager, even."

"I concur," said the Steel Butterfly.

"Is there any way to defuse the device?" asked Constantine.

"Cupid says no," replied Attila.

"What would happen if a military ship made a direct hit on Simon Gold's ship?"

"Cupid says that he's got the detonator tied into his ship's life-support system," answered Attila. "The second the system goes, the device explodes."

"I see," said Constantine. "What are the chances that we can get everyone off the *Comet* in the next few hours?"

"I don't know," answered the Security chief.

"What's *your* opinion?" he asked the Steel Butterfly.

She shrugged. "I think he'll trigger the device before he lets a single member of the crew off the *Comet*."

Constantine frowned. "I'll get back to you," he said, and suddenly his image vanished.

When the deadline was six hours away, Attila contacted Simon again.

"Have you decided to allow our patrons to leave?" he asked.

"All but ten," replied Simon.

"Which ten?"

"It makes no difference to me," said Simon. "*You* choose them."

"If you don't care who they are, why not let them all go?" demanded Attila.

"Because I want every one of your customers to know that it could just as easily have been him or her—and I want the ten to know that they are still in jeopardy as a result of *your* choice, not mine." He paused. "I happen to know that you currently have seven hundred and twenty-six customers aboard the *Comet*. Before I will permit them to leave, I want to tie my computer into the terminal at your airlock. If more than seven hundred and sixteen people pass through, I'll detonate the device immediately. I've made my peace with God; it makes no difference to me whether I die now or in six more hours."

Attila broke the connection.

"Cupid?"

"Yes, Attila."

"Are there any patrons currently in the hospital?"

"Yes, Attila. There are two."

"Are either of them ambulatory?"

"Not at present."

"All right. Get me Cordero."

"Yes, sir?" said the green-clad Security man a moment later.

Attila explained Simon's terms for the evacuation to him. "Have Cupid pick eight names at random," he concluded, "and detain them. Then have the staff oversee the evacuation, and keep it as orderly as possible."

He then contacted the Steel Butterfly and told her what was happening.

"I've heard from Constantine twice more," she informed him. "He couldn't keep the details from the Navy, and now the news media have got their hands on it too."

"Wonderful," muttered Attila. "I wonder how many psychotics are flying up here to help him."

"The Navy's cordoned off the area, but they've agreed not to move in as long as we're trying to negotiate with him."

"Which means until he pushes the button, at which time the negotiations are over.

He broke the connection, poured himself a cup of coffee, checked periodically on the evacuation, had three more futile conversations with Constantine and two with his subordinates, and waited.

When there were only two hours remaining, Constantine put through yet another call.

"Any change in the situation?" he asked.

"None."

"He's playing his cards awfully well, I'll give him that," said Constantine.

"Has anyone at Vainmill decided what we're going to do about him?"

"We're working on it," replied Constantine. "Sit tight a little longer. The Navy is still studying his position."

"You want to know his position?" said Attila. "I'll tell you his position. He's positioned in the goddamned control chair with his thumb about two inches away from the detonation button!"

"Keep calm."

"If you think I'm nervous now, try me again in an hour and a half!" snapped Attila.

"I'm going to have one last talk with him, and

then I'll make a decision," said Constantine. "Have the computer patch me through again."

His image instantly appeared above Simon's computer.

"This is Richard Constantine again."

"You've got less than two hours," Simon announced.

"Will you consider a counterproposal?"

"No," said Simon serenely. He broke the connection.

"He's crazy, you know that?" complained Constantine. "He's gone farther over the edge than his father!"

A light flashed on his desk, and he activated another computer screen, read a message, and looked up at Attila. "The Navy says that there's no possibility of boarding his ship before he can detonate the device."

"I could have told you that six hours ago," said Attila.

"Keep the communication open," said Constantine, getting to his feet. "I'll be back in a couple of minutes."

He walked out of camera range, and Attila spent the next five minutes staring at his empty office. Then he returned and sat back down at his desk.

"I'm told that we have a number of escape pods aboard the ship in case of severe meteor damage," said Constantine. "How may people could they hold if we were to jettison them during a last minute military attack?"

Attila checked with Cupid.

"Six hundred," he replied.

"And the *Comet* is carrying six hundred and nineteen," mused Constantine.

"Plus ten patrons."

Constantine lowered his head in thought for a long moment, then looked up.

"All right," he said with a sigh of defeat. "He wins." He paused. "I suppose you might as well put me through to him."

His image appeared above Simon's computer once more.

"This is Richard Constantine. We will meet your demands."

"Good," said Simon. He checked the time. "You've got ninety-six minutes to get all the employees off the *Velvet Comet*. They can use the customer's ships."

"Just a minute," said Constantine. "This is a deal, not a capitulation. What do *you* intend to do once they've left the *Comet*?"

"I'll monitor broadcast transmissions from Deluros VIII," replied Simon. "As soon as I hear an acceptable number of stations that are not owned by Vainmill announce that the *Comet* has been permanently decommissioned, I'll return to the planet and turn myself over to the authorities."

"You won't try to escape?"

Simon smiled triumphantly. "I fear only God, not men."

The *Velvet Comet's* second evacuation began ten minutes later, and three minutes before Simon's deadline was up, Attila and the Steel Butterfly became the last two personnel to leave it.

Simon waited until half a dozen broadcasts had confirmed the fact, then headed back to Deluros VIII, totally unconcerned about what the future held for him, secure in the knowledge that the God of Thomas Gold was proud of him.

19

A week had passed.

Simon Gold, who had been taken into custody immediately upon his return to Deluros VIII, was awaiting trial.

More than one hundred patrons had filed lawsuits against the Vainmill Syndicate and the *Velvet Comet*.

And the Steel Butterfly had been trying, without success, to see Richard Constantine.

When the call came through that he was finally willing to grant her an audience, she left the hotel that housed the *Comet's* staff, took a monorail to the Vainmill Building, and was soon sitting in the reception room of his 103rd-floor suite. She waited for half an hour, and was ushered into his office.

"You're looking well," he said, remaining seated and gesturing to her to sit down.

"I may be looking well, but I'm *feeling* ignored," she said. "Do you know how long I've been trying to see you?"

"I apologize," he replied insincerely. "I've been quite busy. What can I do for you?"

"You know why I'm here. Simon Gold's been in jail for a week and his father is locked away in some asylum, so I want to know when you're re-opening the *Comet* for business."

"We're not."

"I had a feeling that would be your answer," she said. "May I ask why not?"

"A number of reasons," replied Constantine. "There's lack of customer confidence, for one thing; the *Comet* caters to the wealthiest men and women in the Republic, and we'd have a difficult time convincing them that we could protect them. And, of course, there's Simon Gold."

"You can't seriously expect me to believe that he's not going to spend the next twenty or thirty years in jail."

"Oh, he'll be incarcerated for at least that long," said Constantine. "But he's still the leader of his church, and we've somehow blundered into doing the one thing we most wanted to avoid: we've turned him into a martyr." He paused. "If we reopen the *Comet* for business, how long do you think it will take him to exhort his followers to do exactly what *he* did? And this time there would be no bargaining with them."

"Then spend some of your trillions of credits on external security. Make sure that no armed vessel can approach us."

"It has often been said than no man is safe from an assassin who is willing to sacrifice his own life. The same is true of the *Comet*. To make it completely secure from the kind of fanatics who would be coming after it would cost more money than the operation brings in." He paused. "No, the best thing to do is close the books on it and be grateful that everyone escaped with his life."

"And at least one of us escaped with his career," she added caustically.

"You misunderstand the purpose of this meeting," he answered her calmly. "I didn't call you in to announce the death of the *Comet*, but the birth of six hundred and nineteen new careers. Vainmill always takes care of its own. Everyone who worked aboard the *Comet* was under contract, and we intend to honor those contracts. Attila and his staff will be provided with jobs aboard our luxury spaceliners, as will the technical crew."

"And what about the prostitutes? We're the ones who actually made your profit for you."

"Well, that *is* a somewhat awkward situation," he replied. "As you know, the *Velvet Comet* was Vainmill's only venture into prostitution, and based on our experience we don't anticipate ever so venturing again. Still, we feel a deep sense of responsibility toward you and your staff—"

"Especially since our contracts are still valid," she interjected.

"So we've taken the liberty of making a rather unusual arrangement," he concluded, completely unruffled by her comment.

"What arrangement?" she asked suspiciously.

"You are aware of the training school on Delvania?"

"Of course."

"Well, with the *Comet* decommissioned there is obviously no longer any need for a school. But we've spoken to Suma, and offered her substantial financing at very favorable rates to turn her school into a working brothel—on the condition that she offer employment to any member of your staff who desires it."

"On Delvania?"

"Yes."

"Have you ever *been* to Delvania?" she asked.

"I can't say that I've had that pleasure."

"Then let me tell you about it," said the Steel Butterfly. "It's dry, it's dusty, it's dirty, it's under-populated, and in winter you can fry an egg on the street—if you can *find* a street. You can't expect men and women who have worked in the most luxurious setting in the Republic to voluntarily move to Delvania!"

"The choice is theirs," said Constantine with an unconcerned shrug.

"None of them will go."

"Well, I'm not Simon the Eradicator," he said. "I can't hold a gun to their heads and *force* them to go. But if they don't," he added, "Vainmill will consider their contracts to be terminated, and will feel itself under no further obligation to them."

"Why are you doing this?" she asked, honestly puzzled. "You've been looking for a reason to kill the *Comet* ever since Fiona Bradley put you in charge of Entertainment and Leisure."

"Candidly? I like my money in banks and bonds and investments. I get very nervous seeing it parading around on the hoof, the way it did on the *Comet*. You put that many billionaires in that kind of setting and it's an open invitation to disaster. If it wasn't Thomas and Simon Gold this year, it would have been somebody else next year. To he honest, I'm surprised it took this long to happen."

"What will become of it now?" she asked.

"The *Comet*? We'll sell off the furniture and

whatever else we can. I suppose the shell will go into drydock."

"It was a fabulous institution," she said sadly. "It deserved better."

"It's been my observation that people—and objects—tend to get what they deserve," replied Constantine. "Two months from now every patron it had will have found some other recreational outlet. A year from now no one will even think of it. And ten years from now you'll have to look it up in a history book to know it existed."

"Well, you're a very bright man, Mr. Constantine," she said, "so I suppose you're right. But, damn it, you shouldn't be!"

The Steel Butterfly returned to her hotel room and drank a final bittersweet toast to the ship that had fulfilled so many fantasies for almost a century.

Then, with a sigh of resignation, she turned to the task of securing gainful employment for the last madam of the *Velvet Comet*.

EPILOGUE

The tall, gaunt man, his clothes dusty with the wind-blown dirt of the Delvanian streets, stood before the large, ancient building for a moment, checked the address he had scribbled down in a small notebook, and cautiously entered through the front door.

A frail old woman, confined to a wheelchair, sat behind a reception desk.

"Welcome to Suma's," she said in a quavering voice. Then she smiled. "*I'm* Suma."

He stared at her, but made no move to approach her.

"Can I help you?" she asked.

"I don't know," he replied nervously, and she noticed that his hands were shaking.

Suma smiled at him. "Why do I think that this is your first visit to a whorehouse?"

"Because it is," he whispered.

"There's no need to be nervous about it," she said with a chuckle. "I've been watching them come and go for more than seventy years. You wouldn't believe it to look at me now, but I was very beautiful once."

"I'm sure you were."

"I was," she repeated. "Did you ever hear of the *Velvet Comet?* You know, that place they closed up a few years back?" She waited for a reaction, but saw only increased nervousness. "Well, once upon a time I was its madam." She peered at him intently. "Don't I know you?"

He shook his head abruptly. "I told you—this is my first time."

"Not from here," she said. "From somewhere else. Were you ever on the video?" He made no answer, and she shrugged. "Well, how many video stars come out here anyway?" She paused. "Won't you step a little closer? My eyes aren't as good as they used to be. I can barely see you." She stared at him again. "My, but you're pale! Where have you been hiding yourself?"

"I've been sick," he said carefully.

"Well, you're healthy now, and that's all we care about," she said.

"Before we go any farther, I want your assurances that this establishment is discreet."

She chuckled again. "We're on Delvania. How much more discreet can we be than that?"

"I wasn't being facetious!" he snapped.

"Neither was I," she replied seriously. She stared at him again. "You know, I could swear I've seen you before!"

"I very much doubt it." He looked annoyed. "Are these questions necessary?"

"Not at all," she said. "Let's get right down to business. What did you have in mind?"

"I wish to rent a companion for the night."

"We've got a large assortment on hand," she replied. "Have you any preference?"

The gaunt man's eyes shone with a strange excitement that almost frightened her.

"Something *small*," he said.

About the Author

MIKE RESNICK was born in Chicago in 1942, attended the University of Chicago (where, in the process of researching his first adventure novel, he earned three letters on the fencing team and was nationally ranked for a brief period), and married his wife, Carol, in 1961. They have one daughter, Laura.

From the time he was 22, Mike has made his living as a professional writer. He and Carol have also been very active at science fiction conventions, where Mike is a frequent speaker and Carol's stunning costumes have swept numerous awards at masquerade competitions.

Mike and Carol were among the leading breeders and exhibitors of show collies during the 1970s, a hobby which led them to move to Cincinnati and purchase a boarding and grooming kennel.

Mike has received several awards for his short stories and an award for a nonfiction book for teenagers. His first love, though, remains science fiction, and his excellent science fiction novels—THE SOUL EATER, BIRTHRIGHT: THE BOOK OF MAN, WALPURGIS III, SIDESHOW, THE THREE-LEGGED HOOTCH DANCER, THE WILD ALIEN TAMER, THE BEST ROOTIN' TOOTIN' SHOOTIN' GUNSLINGER IN THE WHOLE DAMNED GALAXY, THE BRANCH, and the first two books in the TALES OF THE VELVET COMET series, EROS ASCENDING and EROS AT ZENITH—are also available in Signet editions.

Signet brings the stars to you . . .

Where no man has gone before . . .